DELIVERANCE
Justice Belstrang Mysteries: Book Three


John Pilkington

# CONTENTS

DELIVERANCE

# ONE

The Great Comet first appeared in the southern sky about the sixth day of September, in the year 1618. With hindsight, I might say it marked the beginning of a period of disruption in my otherwise peaceful life, on my modest acres at Thirldon. For many, the object was seen as a portent, called by some the 'angry star' because of its reddish hue. Small good could come of such an omen, Worcestershire folk said – not least my own steward Childers.

'It bodes ill, Master Justice,' he insisted, as the two of us walked in the garden on a balmy Sabbath evening. 'See now, what of the war on the Continent? Our own King could find himself caught up in it, and what might follow from that?'

'It's hardly a war,' I told him. 'Some angry Protestants in Prague threw some Catholic envoys out of a window. It's what they seem to do in Bohemia – "defenestration" it's called.' But seeing his sober expression, I added: 'I feel sure the King will keep out of the business. He has no wish to lose his reputation as the Peacemaker.'

'Even though his own daughter is married to the ruler of that country?' Childers countered.

I had to admit that his point was apt. Since her marriage five years before to the young Elector Frederick, the Princess Elizabeth might indeed find herself affected by the troubles in Middle Europe. Though here in balmy Worcestershire, where news was somewhat slow in arriving, we had heard only vague rumours of unrest.

'Let us hope for the best,' I said lamely; my stomach was too full of beef and claret to allow unease to arise. 'One day, perhaps, these fearful tussles between the two religions may be a relic of the past. I certainly hope so.'

But Childers shook his head. 'I fear that day will be very far off, sir – if it ever comes.'

We walked back to the house, pondering the matter. England had been at peace for almost a decade, since the Dutch Truce of 1609. But who knew when conflict might erupt again? The Treaty would expire in another three years, and already there was talk of certain factions rearming. Striving to put such matters aside, I gave Childers goodnight and was making my way to my private closet to read Tacitus, when I was accosted in the hallway by a delegation of Thirldon people – or two of them at least: Henry my cook, and Lockyer my manservant.

'What is it?' I asked, seeing they had the appearance of men on a mission. 'I'm about to retire for the night.'

'Your pardon, Master Justice,' Lockyer began. 'We would like to ask your permission to be absent, tomorrow afternoon.'

'To go into Worcester,' Henry added.

'Indeed? For what purpose?' I enquired.

'The matter is, there's to be a play, in the yard at the King's Head,' Lockyer answered. 'The Earl of Arundel's players are come. It should be a splendid show - our last chance to see them on their summer tour.'

On a sudden, I felt inclined to laugh. These two strong men – Henry the scourge of the kitchens, and Lockyer the fearless ex-soldier – now looked like boys suppressing their excitement at a possible treat. 'Well, seeing as it's your last chance, I had best allow it,' I said… whereupon a thought struck me. 'Are you asking for yourselves, or on behalf of others?'

A sheepish look appeared on Henry's face, but Lockyer spoke up. 'In truth, I understand everyone would like to go, sir,' he said stiffly. 'Save Dickon who's too deaf, and Sarah who thinks play-acting is sinful.'

He named the oldest gardener and the washerwoman, which was small surprise. I thought of Hester, and wondered whether she knew of the players coming to Worcester.

'So… the import of your request is that I should give almost my entire household an afternoon's holiday – on a Monday too,' I said, keeping my face free of expression. 'Is that so?'

'It's washing-day,' Henry said hopefully. 'Sarah will still be here to do her work…'

'And Dickon will mind the yard and stables,' Lockyer put in.

'What of Master Childers?' I had assumed my magistrate's tone, which caused both men's faces to fall. 'Have you approached him with your request?'

'We… we thought Master Childers would prefer to remain here, in charge of the house,' Henry answered.

I made no reply; laughter was bubbling up, which I was at some pains to control. Childers regarded plays as frivolous, and all travelling players as rogues.

'So now we have it,' I said. 'Thirldon is to be all but deserted, while my servants decamp *en masse* for the King's Head Inn to idle the afternoon away, abandoning their work.'

'I've made a venison pie for tomorrow's dinner,' Henry said in a forlorn voice - which broke my restraint. In spite of myself, I let out a gasp.

'Lord above, then how can I refuse?' I spluttered – and when both men's faces lit up, I gave way to laughter.

'Then you will allow it, sir?' Lockyer asked, a smile appearing. 'That will be most welcome news.'

'No doubt,' I said, wiping my eye. 'But mind this: I expect everyone to make their way homewards after the play - no lingering at the inn.'

'Of course.' Henry was grinning from ear to ear. 'Now, with your leave I'll return to my domain.'

I waved him away, fumbling for a kerchief. But when Lockyer made his bow and turned to go, I stayed him. 'Do you know what play the Earl's men are performing?'

'I do, sir - it's *Doctor Faustus* by the late Master Marlowe. It's got devils running around, and magic.' He threw me a sly

3

look. 'Not real magic, that is… no harm in a show, is there?'

Summoning a frown, I dismissed him. It seemed unlikely that he was referring to my brush with the supposed witch Agnes Mason the year before, whom I had saved from the gallows. But Thirldon had always been a hive of gossip. My authority, I reflected ruefully, was a mere shadow of what it had been in my magistrate's days. As if to drive the notion home, I had barely retired to my bed-chamber that night when the door opened and Hester entered, wrapped in her russet night-gown.

'If it's about the play tomorrow, I've already been waylaid and given my consent,' I told her. 'I was feeling magnanimous, I suppose… or drowsy with claret-'

'I would like to go too,' Hester interrupted. 'I haven't seen a play in a long time – nor have you.'

Standing in my stockings in the candlelight, I made a gesture of dismissal. 'I've seen *Doctor Faustus* twice, in London,' I said. 'I've no desire to see it again. You should go - you can keep an eye on the Thirldon men, see they don't get soused and start a fight.'

'You wish me to attend alone?' She raised an eyebrow. 'There are no private gallery-boxes at the King's Head. I'd be a target for any lecherous gallant who had a mind to seize me.'

'What piffle,' I muttered, stifling a yawn. 'You'd be a match for any of them.' But there was truth in her words. The inn-yard could be rowdy - and a woman alone, whatever her age, was generally considered fair game…

'In any case, it's likely some of your friends will be there,' Hester said.

'I don't have friends nowadays,' I lied. My old companion Doctor Budge was a true friend, but he was away for the summer spending time with his daughter and her family. 'More likely I'd run into some old enemy from my days on the bench.'

'I believe an afternoon's entertainment will be good for you,' came the reply. 'You never go anywhere, save fishing.'

I sighed. 'May we leave this for the morning?'

'I suppose we may. In fact, that was my thought too.'

She made no move to leave the room; our eyes met, and I drew a sharp breath. 'I see,' I said, in a different tone. 'Is this a matter of bribery, or…?'

'Call it what you will,' Hester said, undoing her gown.

And that was how we both came to be attending a performance at the King's Head Inn, the following afternoon.

It was what followed afterwards, however, that set the cat among the pigeons.

\*\*\*

In spite of my reservations, I had enjoyed the play. The Earl of Arundel's company were seasoned players who had been touring the provinces, and their delivery was well-honed and lively. Though Marlowe's work was familiar to me, I had almost forgotten the power of his poetry, which more than compensated for the knockabout scenes of clowning, to a man of my tastes. The inn-yard was packed, my own servants dotted among the crowd, delighting in the show. As did Hester, who was moved by the cries of the wretched Faustus when the devils come to drag him off to hell at the end. She spoke of it as we made our way out through the throng and into the street.

'It's a morality tale - one of straight retribution,' I told her. 'If you make a pact with evil, you pay the price. As for yearning after Helen of Troy – or even her spirit – that's mere lust personified.'

'Of course - Master Justice,' she replied, with a dour look. 'Being a paragon of virtue yourself, you naturally disapprove of pleasure for its own sake.'

I lowered my gaze; having enjoyed a rare episode of carnality with her the previous night, I was in no position to preach. We walked on in silence through the busy street, past the Guildhall where, on a sudden, Hester stopped.

'Do you see who it is?' She asked, tugging my sleeve.

I looked up, and drew to a halt myself. Walking towards us was Dorothy Standish, the wife of my old rival Justice Matthew Standish, with whom I had oft been at loggerheads. Especially in the previous year, when I'd had a hand in the downfall of the wicked landowner Giles Cobbett, friend and – so I had deduced – silent paymaster of the unscrupulous Justice. I never saw Standish, as a rule. He and I were enemies, now that I knew he had been one of those responsible for my having to quit as magistrate. Nor had I any wish to speak to his haughty wife. I took Hester's arm and would have walked past her – but to my surprise the woman blocked our path. Only then did I notice that she was not alone, but in the company of an over-dressed gallant who must have been twenty years her junior.

'Master Belstrang…' a thin smile appeared. 'How pleasant to see you… you and your servant.'

'Madam.' I managed the curtest of nods. 'Your pardon, but we cannot stay.'

'Of course you can't… always such a busy man.' The lady half-turned to her companion - a simpering fellow, I surmised. 'Master Belstrang was once a Justice here, did you know?' She murmured. 'Now he… well, in truth I'm not sure what it is he does now. Tends his fruit trees, perhaps?'

Beside me, I felt Hester stiffen. Suppressing a retort, I made as if to side-step the two of them, but it seemed Mistress Standish was not done with me yet.

'It's such a pity,' she said sweetly. 'You have my deepest condolences for your coming loss. The Justice and I were most saddened when we heard.'

'I don't follow you,' I said, feeling a frown coming on. 'Pray, what is this loss you speak of?'

'I quite understand,' came the reply. 'It must be too painful to speak of... I'm most sorry for raising the matter.'

'What matter?' Hester asked. She shifted her gaze from Mistress Standish's face to that of her foppish friend, who curled his lip disdainfully. But now, having chosen her moment, the lady delivered her killing blow.

'Why, the loss of Thirldon, of course,' she said, lifting her brows at me. 'It's tragic... your family have dwelt there for generations, have they not? But then, when the eye of His Majesty the King lights on such a prize, there's little one can do, is there?'

I gazed at her, too stunned to speak. Beside me, Hester jerked as if struck.

'God in heaven, Madam, do you not see what you have done?' The perfumed popinjay on Mistress Standish's arm spoke up in a languid tone. 'I'd lay odds the poor man doesn't know yet... he's plain lost his reason, along with his voice!'

'Oh, my dear...' Mistress Standish put on a look of such horror, she could have done sterling work as a player. Lifting a hand, she made as if to ward off the thought. 'But this is unbearable, sir – I naturally assumed that you knew!'

And she would have put a consoling palm out to me, had I not received a dig in the ribs from Hester. In a moment she had drawn me aside, ushering me away from this cruel-hearted woman. I was still so shaken by her words that I submitted, the pair of us almost stumbling off up the street, jostled by the throng still coming from the play. After taking a few paces, however, I stopped and turned back, as if to reassure myself of what had just occurred.

There, watching me with a shameless smirk, stood Mistress Standish. To add further insult her companion swept off his hat and made a bow, then burst into mocking laughter.

'Come, walk!'

Hester gripped my arm, urging me onward. With an effort, I

7

picked up my pace and walked with her until we had put some distance between ourselves and the people who had spoiled our afternoon so harshly. Not until we had reached the stables where our mounts awaited us, did we pause for breath.

'Surely you didn't believe her?' She faced me, her eyes full of concern. 'She meant to dismay you, nothing more. She has never forgiven you for getting the better of her husband as you did last year… she is bitterness itself!'

I exhaled, and gave a nod. 'But what an odd thing to say. Can such a rumour truly have got around? In God's name, how can that be?'

'It's nonsense. Rumours may come from nothing – a few words slurred by someone in drink. It was said to spite you.'

'But…' I found myself frowning. 'You recall what might have happened to John Jessop, when he almost lost Sackersley? Once the King takes a fancy to some pleasant country manor, for one reason or another-'

'For pity's sake!' Hester exclaimed. 'The King has never set foot in this county – I doubt he's even heard of Thirldon.'

'Well… perhaps,' I allowed. Letting out another long breath, I gestured to the stable doors. 'Let's get ourselves home, shall we? I need a drink of something.'

But Hester remained still, looking hard at me.

'The idea is preposterous,' she insisted. 'And I dislike the thought of riding back with you working yourself into a turmoil over it. I say again - it's pure nonsense.'

But it was not.

I arrived home to find that a letter had been delivered, sent in haste from my son-in-law George Bull in London, advising me of grave news that had been brought to his attention.

It seemed King James was about to make me an offer of purchase for Thirldon: the house and the entire estate, to gift to his favourite the Marquis of Buckingham. Naturally, it was assumed that I would humbly accept this honour bestowed by the King, and make arrangements to suit.

Whereupon Mistress Standish's words rang in my head: *When the eye of His Majesty lights on such a prize, there's little one can do, is there?*

## TWO

To say that there was consternation in my house that evening, would be a gross understatement.

Childers, in some ways, took the news even more to heart than I did. Thirldon was all he knew, having spent his entire life in my family's service. Whereas one of my first thoughts was for the rest of the servants. Fortunately, it appeared that none of them had heard of the matter, even in Worcester. How Mistress Standish came to be in early possession of such knowledge, was food for much thought.

'Even George is dismayed,' I said, holding up his letter. We sat in my private chamber, Hester, Childers and I, fortified with cups of strong sack. 'He says the King can refuse Buckingham nothing. His Lordship is Master of Horse now, atop all his other titles, and likely set for a dukedom. Building up estates in Ireland, it seems, though what gave him the idea of adding Thirldon to his properties I'm uncertain...'

I broke off, as a notion sprang up; indeed, it had been at the back of my mind since the return journey from Worcester.

'Standish,' Hester said, divining my thoughts as she so often did. 'He must have had a hand in this.'

I gazed at her, even as Childers let out a sigh. 'It would explain what his wife said to you in the town, sir,' he muttered, with a shake of his head. 'By all that's holy...'

We were silent for a while. Hester was shaken, but remained calm. 'The man must burn with revenge, after you thwarted him last year,' she said after a while. 'He's acquainted with important men – as is his wife. That woman would use any means to hurt us. She could even have spread the word about Thirldon's desirability herself.'

'It may be so,' I breathed.

A great weight had settled upon me. I turned my attention to

George's letter again, re-reading it for perhaps the third time. He had learned of the King's intention to purchase Thirldon from another lawyer who was well versed in Court affairs, and was doing his best to find out more. Meanwhile his wife, my beloved daughter Anne, was distraught at the thought of losing our family estate. The two of them assured me that, should matters go as we feared, Hester and I would have a home with them for as long as we wished. Lifting my gaze, I repeated the offer to the others.

'Why, it sounds as if we are to become homeless,' Hester said. 'I've heard the King can be parsimonious, but surely he would offer a fair price for the estate?'

'He might offer it,' I told her. 'But when, or even if he would pay up, is another matter entirely.'

Childers let out a long breath; he was looking even older than his years, which were approaching seventy. 'The Great Comet,' he said gloomily. 'I knew it boded ill – I said so, did I not?'

'That's fluff and flummery,' Hester retorted. But her eyes were on the floor, and the words carried little conviction. Once again we lapsed into silence, until with an effort I managed to summon some spirit.

'See now, it's not done yet,' I said. 'There will be papers to draw up... George Bull is an able man, and not without influence. He offers to petition the King on my behalf, which would at least spare me travelling to London, cap in hand. The business could be delayed, at least long enough for me to find some other suitable property, not far away. Even if it comes to renting-'

'By God, sir!' At that, Childers looked aghast. 'Are you to be reduced to house-hunting? It's intolerable, for a gentleman of your standing...' He trailed off, struggling to master himself. And even Hester, who was sometimes impatient with my oldest

11

servant, was moved to pity him.

'I cannot believe it will come to that,' she said. 'Master Justice will speak with friends from his Inns of Court days... there must be some who can offer advice. Is it not so?'

Meeting her gaze, I managed a nod. 'Indeed... I will begin writing letters, first thing tomorrow. Including to Sir Samuel Sandys – why should I not? Our High Sheriff is a man of ability and integrity. He may be able to shed some light on the matter... or then again, he may not.'

I paused, glancing at each of them in turn. 'In the meantime, nothing must be said to the servants about this,' I added. 'All should appear as normal – I'll not have them distressed. If anyone has heard a rumour, it must be denied with force. I'm counting on you both.'

We exchanged looks, but there was no need for further words. When it came to Hester and Childers, my trust was as firm as it had always been. Soon afterwards we went to our beds, but I doubt if either of them slept, any more than I did. How the coming days and weeks would pass, we could not know.

But two days later I was interrupted at my desk to receive another letter, of a very different nature to the one from my son-in-law. I had no inkling then that it would prove to be pivotal with regard to my future - but so it was.

***

It was Wednesday, and I seemed to have done little but send out messages since the fateful news had arrived from George. Naturally I asked him to petition the King as he had offered, and to keep me abreast of all that occurred. I also wrote to lawyers who had been fellow-students in my days at Gray's Inn, though with little hope that they could offer any assistance. Hence, I was somewhat irritated by the distraction of hearing from a friend I had not seen in years: Sir Richard Mountford, a landowner who lived downriver, near the village of Upton. He and I had little in common these days, Mountford having invested heavily in such commodities as iron ore and timber, by which means he had built a substantial fortune. My first thought, preoccupied as I was, had been to set his letter aside, until I saw the black tags which adorned it. So I broke the seal, and read the sad news: Mountford's younger brother John, whom I too had known, was dead, killed in a tragic accident. The man was broken with grief, and appeared to be reaching out to those he knew, for whatever comfort they might offer.

At dinner I showed the letter to Hester. Childers was elsewhere, striving to keep himself busy; it was all he could do, to ward off the gloom that threatened to overwhelm him.

'Mountford invites me to visit his manor, Foxhill,' I said. 'It's impossible just now, of course... I can only send him my condolences.'

'It's only a two-hour ride away,' Hester said, alert on a sudden. 'The diversion would take your mind off your troubles. Surely you've written to everyone you know by now?'

'I suppose so... but I'm hardly the one to cheer a bereaved man at such a time. We would merely be fellows in misery.'

'He's in want of a sympathetic ear,' Hester said. 'You can offer that, at least. It's precisely the distraction you need, instead of losing sleep and fretting while George acts on your behalf in London.'

As always, she was winning the argument. And now that I turned the matter about, there was nothing to prevent me riding down to Upton to spend a day or two. I took up Mountford's letter again and looked at the final paragraph... then gave a start as I read his parting words.

'Good God.' I raised my eyes to Hester's. 'The man fears that he too is dying, though he does not say why.'

'Then that settles it,' she replied. 'You must go to him... he would value your presence.'

I dropped the letter on the table. 'Yes... his troubles are far worse than mine. I suppose the two of us can get drunk, at least.'

\*\*\*

I left Thirldon the following morning, riding Leucippus at a steady pace into Worcester, then southwards on the old Tewkesbury road. The day was fair, and as Hester had suggested, it was a relief to feel the breeze as I rode, and to clear my mind of worry for a while. The harvest was in train, men toiling in the fields as I passed. Striving to put aside thoughts of Thirldon and the King's desire to take it from me, I began to recall Richard Mountford in the days when we were drinking companions in London, long before he had been knighted. He was good company, a jovial fellow who generally took things in his stride; the contrast between the man I remembered and the tone of his letter was stark. Then, grief may enfeeble the stoutest of hearts; like me he was a widower, and doubtless the loss of his brother, with whom he had always been close, was a severe blow. I hoped that his son, whom I had not seen since he was a boy, was of some comfort to him.

On that score, however, I was about to be disillusioned.

I arrived in Upton towards mid-day, having crossed the old stone bridge to the Severn's west bank, where the village fronted the river. A mile or so of further riding brought me to the sprawling manor of Foxhill, set amid woods where deer browsed and fields where sheep grazed. It was a fine house, wide-fronted, gabled and imposing; Mountford had done well for himself. In the courtyard I was met by a servant in livery, who called a stable-boy to take care of Leucippus. Then I was escorted indoors - to be greeted not by my old friend, but by a tall, well-groomed man who announced himself as his son Francis.

'I'm confounded, sir,' I said, taking his hand. 'The last time I saw you, you were a lad of thirteen or fourteen years.'

'Is that so, sir? I confess I do not remember.' Francis Mountford eyed me, somewhat coolly I thought, and dropped my hand. 'A good deal of water has flowed under the bridge since then.'

I looked him over, noting a tautness in his manner. 'That's true. But pray, how does Sir Richard? I'm eager to see him.'

'In truth, he's unwell,' Francis replied. 'He sees few people at present. My wife and I have urged him to rest, given the dreadful blow he has suffered, with my uncle's untimely death.'

'Of course...' I stiffened slightly. Instead of welcoming me as a friend of his father's, who might offer some cheer, this man seemed almost to disapprove of my coming.

'So, you are married?' I made an effort to smile. 'I'm eager to meet your good lady.'

'And you shall, sir,' the other said briskly. 'Now, I understand you have been invited to stay with us, hence a chamber has been made ready. Would you like to make yourself comfortable, before joining us at dinner?'

'Gladly,' I answered. 'But might I attend Sir Richard first?'

'He is sleeping, sir.'

This time there was little doubt: Francis Mountford's tone was forbidding, if not quite hostile. I met his eye until, with some effort, he assumed an easier manner.

'I meant not to dissuade you,' he said. 'It's better we wait until after our dinner, when he will be recovered. I will tell a servant to advise him of your arrival.'

'Very well...' I gave a nod, glancing about the well-appointed hall with its hangings and display of fine plate. Iron mines and timber, it seemed, had paid for all of this. I was still mulling over the matter as I was led upstairs to my chamber, with its eastward view towards the town. On the landing I had passed a number of doors, all closed. Behind one of them, it would appear, Sir Richard Mountford was sleeping - at mid-day. Was that, I wondered, the cause of the unease on my part?

I decided to put a few questions to his son over dinner.

It was a sumptuous meal, which far exceeded my appetite. Francis and his wife Maria were good hosts, clearly accustomed to entertaining on a grand scale. Attentive servants hovered, ready to refill my cup at any moment until I declined. Meanwhile I observed the couple, especially Mistress Mountford: a delicate, fair-haired young woman of pale complexion, with deep-set eyes.

'I understand you have put aside the burdens of a magistrate, Master Belstrang,' she said, peering at me over the rim of her silver chalice. 'That must be a relief.'

'Some years ago, Madam,' I replied. 'But that's not how I view it. I believe I may yet be of service to our county.'

'Is it so?' The lady raised an eyebrow. 'I would have thought that, as a man of similar age to my father-in-law, you would appreciate having the time to enjoy your estate.'

'I do. But I also try to occupy myself when I can.'

Francis gave a perfunctory nod of approval. 'Your sentiments do you justice, sir.'

'And what of Sir Richard?' I enquired, keen to change the topic. 'Does he not enjoy life here at Foxhill? For he has clearly prospered. The timber trade must be proving fruitful.'

'Not nearly so fruitful as the foundries,' Maria Mountford said, with a smile that was close to a smirk. But at once, she appeared to regret her words: her husband's glance was forbidding. Sensing an opening, I spoke up.

'That's most interesting – where are they situated? I hear the Weald of Kent is most abundant with regard to iron.'

'Our family used to have interests there,' Francis said, after a moment's pause. 'We have since transferred business to the Forest of Dean, down in Gloucestershire.'

'It's more discreet,' Maris put in airily, which occasioned

another disapproving glance from her husband.

'Well, I know of the forestry down there,' I said. 'I thought the mines were the lesser industry.'

'The new furnaces have brought great improvement,' Francis replied. 'But they need a lot of charcoal. The proximity of wood and iron ore serves the foundries well.'

'And what do they produce, your foundries?' I asked.

For a moment, however, no reply was forthcoming. I saw Francis catch his wife's eye again. Finally, when the silence had grown somewhat long, he gave his answer.

'Cannons, sir, for His Majesty's armouries. Though it's not something I normally discuss with guests. I would beg your discretion in the matter.'

I allowed my surprise to show. 'Well now, I had no inkling that Sir Richard was involved in such activity.'

'He's one of the King's Founders of Ordnance,' Maria Mountford put in, with another smirk. It struck me that the lady had imbibed somewhat too liberally of the good Gascon wine we had enjoyed. Sensing her husband's growing irritation at her loosening tongue, I was about to make some remark, when a notion sprang up unbidden.

'Your uncle... John Mountford,' I said, turning to Francis. 'Was he too concerned with the casting of guns?'

This time a silence fell, which even the man's spouse did not break. In a very short time, the atmosphere had grown taut. I waited, glancing from one to the other, until Francis chose to enlighten me.

'He was. And the tragedy is, he died while engaged in that very activity, at our works at Lydney. An explosion... a terrible event.' He put on a sombre look. 'The work has always carried risks, as my uncle well knew. It seems harsh that he should have perished in such a manner.'

'It does indeed,' I said. 'Please accept my sympathies.' I drew a breath, and added: 'And now I'm most eager to speak with Sir Richard, to offer him my sympathies.'

Francis nodded, dabbing at his mouth with a napkin. 'I will accompany you forthwith.' He glanced at his wife, then: 'There's no need for you to come up, Madam.'

Maria Mountford had been about to speak, I saw, but at his words she merely pouted; it was another awkward moment. Somewhat wearied by her behaviour, I rose from my chair.

'With your leave, I will await you by the staircase.'

Which I did, standing in the hallway until Francis came out. As we began to ascend the stairs together he spoke readily enough, with an attempt at levity which I found false.

'I pray you'll indulge my wife, sir - she is not quite herself. She is still unnerved by John's death. It's barely a fortnight since the burial... the body was sent upriver by boat, so broken and maimed that we were advised not to view it. I'm sure you understand.'

I gave a nod. 'It must have been a distressing time for all of you. I remember how fond your father was of his brother.'

He said nothing further, but stopped outside a closed door. Unsure what to expect, I now found myself ill-at-ease, which Francis appeared not to notice. He knocked, then opened the door and entered, bidding me follow. The room was dim, heavy drapes covering most of the windows. As my eyes grew accustomed to the gloom, I discerned a great four-poster bed, its curtains drawn. At our appearance, a figure rose abruptly from a stool nearby.

'Is he awake?' Francis asked.

'I believe so, sir.' The elderly servant bobbed quickly. 'Shall I tell him you're come?'

'No, you may leave,' came the terse reply.

In silence the woman walked past us, head lowered. As she went out, closing the door, Francis faced me.

18

'I must beg your discretion, Master Belstrang,' he said, speaking low. 'We take every care not to alarm my father, nor trouble him in any way. Despite the efforts of his physician, he is weak – and, I might add, prone to delirium at times.'

I gave him no reply. My eyes were on the bed, from where I believed I heard a faint stirring of pillows.

'And more…' Francis leaned closer, obliging me to meet his eye. 'We never speak of the accident. It distresses him.'

'Yes, I understand.' With some impatience, I gestured towards the four-poster. 'Well, may I see him now?'

Still the man hesitated, seemingly unwilling to leave me alone. Why was that? But at last, he gave a nod and stepped back.

'I ask you not to stay too long, for discourse tires him,' were his final words. Then he turned and, to my relief, got himself outside. Whereupon, at the sound of the latch, there was a sudden flurry of movement, and the bed-curtains parted.

'Has he gone?' Came a voice, so familiar that it threw me back many years. And when, in mingled surprise and hope, I replied in the affirmative, there came an audible sigh.

'Thanks be to God,' Richard Mountford muttered, even as his head appeared through the gap. 'Now come here, you old dog, and embrace me.'

## THREE

It was an afternoon of surprises.

My first emotion was relief, that my old friend was not as sick as I had feared. He had aged, but no more than I expected for a man of his years. In truth, he appeared a somewhat unlikely invalid.

'I rejoice to see you again,' I told him, when we had done with the greetings. I drew up the servant's stool and sat close. 'I half-expected to find you lying prone – even near to death.'

'Well, I'm not quite the full shilling,' Mountford said, sitting propped against his pillows. 'I had a summer chill, but that passed. I would rather be up and walking the gardens, but I'm ordered to rest. My physician's a dry old stick, who does little but prescribe sleeping draughts. I often pour them into my piss-pot.'

'At least you're being well looked after,' I said, smiling – at which a slight frown appeared.

'Indeed… you might say, too well.'

'Given what you said in your letter, surely no care can be too much?' I replied, with some surprise. 'Do you truly fear you might be close to death?'

'Robert…' he gave a sigh. 'You're a man I trust. I knew that if I expressed such a notion, I could count on your coming here. Hence, I must beg your forgiveness if I exaggerated.'

'So, you are not dying?' I said, after a pause.

'I hope not.' He fell silent for a moment, then: 'In truth, my friend, I need your help. There are few others I could call on just now, with your abilities.'

I confess I was non-plussed; Mountford had always been his own man, decisive and vigorous. But now he appeared troubled: a restless presence, in his sweat-stained night-shirt. I saw uncertainty in his eyes, which was unlike him. I nodded, inviting him to continue.

'My brother John,' he began – and seeing me stiffen, he held up a hand. 'I heard what my son told you, but it's untrue. I'm eager to speak of his death, yet they won't let me. Francis and Maria, I mean... they treat me as if I'm in my dotage.'

There was an edge to his voice now. Lowering his gaze, he added: 'I dislike saying this, but I believe they have designs... secrets...'

He broke off, and I recalled Francis saying that his father was at times *prone to delirium*. Could it be true? Yet I saw no signs of feebleness of mind – only of worry.

'Tell me,' I said. 'If I can aid you, I will.'

He looked up, his relief plain to see, and unburdened himself. 'John's death,' he said heavily. 'I do not believe it was an accident.'

I frowned, but held my peace.

'A clever man, my brother,' he went on. 'He knows – I mean, he knew - the foundries intimately, for he went there often to oversee our properties. Down to Lydney, that is. If there was danger of an explosion, he would have seen it. Besides, we've never had such an incident before.'

I drew a breath. 'You imply-'

'I'm not sure what I imply,' my friend broke in. 'But I'd bet my entire estate that things are being kept from me – by Francis, that is.' He sighed, then: 'I'd have gone down there myself, the moment the news came, summer chill or no. But my son forbade me. John's body was already being shipped up here, on a sailing trow... the captain was a man I know, name of Spry. So I relented; I was downcast, as grief-stricken as I was when my wife died. You know what I speak of.'

I was silent, for I understood - and on a sudden he put out a hand, to grip my arm fiercely.

'Will you look into this matter, Robert? I know it's asking a great deal... perhaps too much, for one of your years. But I know you and, well...' he gave another sigh. 'I feel the reins slipping from my hands - it's driving me to distraction. I need reassurance, that there's not some scheme afoot to edge me towards oblivion!'

And at last, I discerned something in his gaze that I never expected to see: fear, pure and simple. In truth, I saw, my friend was no invalid: he was as good as a prisoner, in his own home. I shifted my hand to return his grip.

'Tell me all you know,' I said. 'Then leave me to act – I'll not rest until I've done my utmost to piece this matter out.'

And so he did, with much relief, the two of us in close conference for a good part of the afternoon. By the time I left him he was in better spirits, though I confess I cannot say the same for myself. Thereafter I spent some time walking in the nearby woods, to settle my mind and make a decision.

Only then did I realise that Mountford's troubles had driven away my own worries about Thirldon. It was something to be thankful for.

\*\*\*

Supper that evening with Francis and Maria Mountford was an uncomfortable affair for me, though neither of them appeared to pay any mind to my demeanour. I was alert, careful not to give away my unease concerning their treatment of Sir Richard. After I had assured Francis that the two of us had spent the afternoon reminiscing about old times, without mention of the death of his uncle, he seemed content to play the benevolent host. But I watched him, wondering what drove this unsmiling man... and what secrets he was keeping from his father.

For I believed my old friend, and found myself eager to get at the truth of what had happened to his brother, far down the River Severn. But if I was to investigate, I thought it wise to do so anonymously – that is, under an invented name. With hindsight I might call it reckless or even foolish, to take the role of a spy. But I needed to busy myself, to keep my fears about Thirldon at a distance. I had formed my resolve, and would stay with it.

Meanwhile, I allowed my hosts to believe that I would return home the following morning.

'So soon, sir?' Maria Mountford murmured languidly. 'What a pity… we understood you to be a keen angler. Francis could have invited you to fish the lake that lies on our land.'

'Alas, I must forgo the pleasure on this occasion,' I replied. Francis made no comment – and now I saw it, plainly enough: he was relieved at the prospect of my departure.

'Can you not at least delay your ride until the afternoon?' His wife persisted. 'As you know, Sir Richard sleeps late… you could take dinner here, then bid him farewell.'

'Much as I would like to, I fear not,' I told her. 'There are matters at home requiring my attention.'

To which the mistress of Foxhill was about to utter some further protest, had she not been silenced by her husband.

'For heaven's sake, Madam,' Francis said sharply. 'Belstrang has stated his intention, and he has his reasons. I pray you, let the man be.' Turning to me, he said smoothly: 'We are delighted to have had your company, sir, which I'm certain will have cheered my father a good deal. You leave with our warmest thanks, and our affection.'

It was all I could do to manage a polite nod. For in truth, my growing dislike for this man had hardened into something else: a deep distrust. I saw no hint of the affection he had spoken of. It merely stiffened my resolve to discover what had happened, down in the distant Forest of Dean.

I left Foxhill early the next day, riding back into Upton where I re-crossed the Severn. But instead of turning northwards towards Worcester, I took the road south towards Tewkesbury.

A much longer ride lay ahead, into a part of rural England I barely knew.

And the man who now set forth on that journey, was no longer ex-magistrate Robert Belstrang of Thirldon: he was William Pride, a man of business. That was my *integumentum* – my cover name, if you will, plucked out of the air. I hoped the diversion would bring results; at the least, it would continue to distract me from fears of losing my home.

\*\*\*

The day was sunny, the early cloud having lifted. Leucippus took the road at a good pace, and we reached the bustling town of Tewkesbury well before mid-day. We had crossed the border into Gloucestershire now, and I stopped to rest the horse, letting him eat from the nose-bag while I took a light dinner at the nearest inn. Here I called for ink and paper, and penned a brief letter to Hester informing her of my intentions, paying the host to send it to Worcester by the first carrier available.

Then I was back in the saddle, crossing the river again on to the road to Tirley. Thereafter it was a steady ride, south-west through the villages of Haffield and Rudford. By late afternoon we were in Westbury, where I watered the horse again. The country was rich and green, yet unfamiliar to me. I pressed on past the great bend in the river, to enter the ancient Forest of Dean. The roads were fewer and narrower now, and I was obliged to stop and ask a carter for directions to Lydney: another four or five miles. Whereupon at last, as evening drew in, I reached the village and drew rein.

It was quiet, little more than a hamlet on the River Lyd, with the great forest at its back. I knew the mills and forges Mountford had described to me were upstream, in the woodlands which stretched away as far as I could see. A track led off towards the Severn, which was but a short distance from here. Tomorrow I would venture forth, posing as a man with money to invest in iron works. But for the moment both Leucippus and I needed rest and sustenance. To my relief there was an inn close by: The Comfort, the sign read. I was soon inside, ordering a room and board and stabling for the horse.

The host was one Henry Hawes, a ruddy-faced Forest of Dean man with an accent I could barely penetrate. But he was courteous, and it was a relief to ease the stiffness from my limbs over a supper and a mug of locally-brewed ale. In response to my casual questions, however, he grew somewhat wary. The Mountford family were indeed well-known, he allowed: one of the biggest employers at their foundries, the nearest being up the Lyd, a mile and a half away. But they were not great landowners hereabouts, like the Catholic Wintours with their noble connections. What, he wondered, was my interest?

I assumed a casual manner, mentioning a small share in iron mines elsewhere, which I might be seeking to increase. William Pride, I decided, should be something of a free-wheeler, prepared to take risks with his money; I believed it would open a few doors. My host having left me to attend to his customers, I finished my drink and surveyed the room, with its thickening fug of tobacco smoke. The drinkers were all working men, downing their ale after a hard day's toil. Feeling wearied, I rose to go to my chamber, only to be accosted by a heavy-bearded fellow in dusty clothes, who barred my way.

'I heard what you were saying to Henry Hawes, sir,' he stated. 'Do you know the Mountfords well?'

I told him I had some slight acquaintance with the family.

'I ask because there's some here would be glad to have news,' the other continued, jerking his thumb over his shoulder. Several other men, I saw, were now looking in my direction. 'Like, when they're likely to get paid again.'

'I'm unable to answer that, my friend,' I told him, with a shrug. 'I'm here to look about, nothing more.'

'Is it so?' The man regarded me, noting my good clothes and my sword, then: 'Foundry business, is it?'

I gave a nod, suppressing my distaste at his impertinent tone; here was a potential source of intelligence. 'Is that your trade?' I asked, and received a nod in return.

'It is. I worked at the Cricklepit Foundry for nigh on ten years – that's Mountford's, under Tobias Russell. Not any longer, though.'

'Might I know your name?'

'Willett, sir. Jonas Willett.'

'Well, Master Willett...' I glanced from him to the other men, who were listening attentively. 'I might pay a visit to that foundry tomorrow, and seek out your old master.' I made no mention of the fact that I already knew the name of Tobias Russell, from my talk with Sir Richard back at Foxhill. 'In the meantime, will you and your friends take a mug with me?' Whereupon I called the host, drew shillings from my purse and handed them over, bidding him serve everyone forthwith.

It was rather un-Belstrang-like, to treat the entire company in such a manner. But I suspected it might prove a good investment.

The next day, however, I would find my initial impression had been a false dawn, with a somewhat rude awakening to follow.

\*\*\*

I did not take Leucippus from the stable, but decided to walk the short distance upstream to the Cricklepit Foundry. The day was cloudy, with a breeze coming up the Severn. In the distance, a woodman's axe rang out as I ventured up the track; the sound would be repeated often, as I walked through the woods. At last, ascending the rushing stream, I reached the mill: a solid, oaken structure with a huge waterwheel. And some distance away stood the foundry: brick-built, with steam issuing from its chimneys. The noise of hammering had been growing louder for the past few minutes, and here was its source: a busy workplace, with men moving about. There were cabins too, and a pen for horses, and nearby a great heap of coarse iron ore.

I stood for a while, taking in the sights and sounds of the foundry, the likes of which I had never seen. Then I remembered why I was here, and grew alert: if this was where the explosion had taken place in which John Mountford had been killed, would there not be some signs of it?

I began to walk towards the main building: the furnace-house, I guessed, from its distinctive shape. Soon I began to feel its heat, and recalled what Francis had said about the process needing a lot of charcoal. Glancing about, I saw one or two men had paused at their work and were eying me curiously. I was about to approach them, when I was challenged abruptly.

'That's far enough, if you please.'

The speaker was a stout man in a thick leather apron. I checked my stride, allowing him to draw near, then assumed a smile.

'Good morning to you... am I addressing Master Russell?'

He halted, looking me over with undisguised suspicion. Finally, having noted my rank, he managed a curt nod.

'You are, sir. But I must ask you to turn about and retrace your steps. The foundry is in the King's service, and not to be visited.'

'Indeed?' I maintained my smile. 'That's unfortunate. I'm acquainted with the owner, Sir Richard Mountford... I have an interest in iron.'

But the other was impassive. 'Even so, you cannot stay. You might apply to the office of the King's Founders of Ordnance.'

'But I've already done so,' I lied, replacing my smile with a look of pained indignation. 'Has no instruction reached you?' And when no answer was returned, I added: 'I am William Pride, from London. I have a share in an iron works in Kent, and am considering investments hereabouts. In truth, I expected a better welcome than this.'

At that, Tobias Russell took a step closer. 'No-one's said anything to me,' he muttered.

'Well, these things take time,' I told him. 'And your habitat is somewhat remote... but there it is. If you insist on turning me away, I'll have to report to my fellow-investors in the city - as well as informing Francis Mountford.'

To my satisfaction, the bluff appeared to work.

'See now, that's not necessary,' Russell said, after a moment. 'If your desire is but to view our workings...' He glanced aside, to where men were still watching, and waved a hand to assure them that all was well. As they went off to their business, he faced me again.

'Investment, you say, sir? Does that mean you intend to establish a new build here, for the casting of iron? The mines are already working to capacity, and the river's power is taxed. You would need to harness another stream.'

For a while I said nothing. Falling into old ways, I met his eye and tried to look behind the gaze... and a notion sprang up.

'It's cannons I'm concerned with,' I said, lowering my voice. 'I have customers waiting – and I do not mean the King. Such trade, as you will know, is most profitable - do I make myself understood?'

But I had erred: I saw it at once, and regretted my words. Instead of approval, I was rebuffed.

'I haven't the least idea what you mean – sir,' Russell answered, his expression hardening. 'And on reflection I'll ask again that you quit this place, and leave me to my work.'

Whereupon he folded his arms and stood, a solid bulk of a man. And William Pride, unscrupulous investor, was obliged to turn about and walk away.

# FOUR

I did not go directly back to the village.

Instead I wandered up the Lyd valley for half a mile or so, and thence up a branching stream - the Newerne, it is called. Here I was surprised to find another iron works almost hidden among the trees, a good deal smaller than Cricklepit. Having drawn close, I found the place occupied by just two men, labouring by a glowing furnace which was visible through the open doors. Half-prepared to be made as unwelcome as I had been earlier, I hailed them from a distance. Then, when one turned about, I recognised him as the man from the inn.

'Jonas Willett?' I stepped forward. 'Well met... I did not expect to find you here, so far upstream.'

'Master Pride, is it?' He came forward, dusting off his hands. He was dripping with sweat, clad in rough clothing and the leather apron common to foundrymen. 'How can I aid you?'

I told him briefly of my visit to Cricklepit, and of my reception. I was curious to note Willett's reaction, and was somewhat surprised by the bitter smile that appeared.

'You'll get nothing out of Russell,' he said. 'Tight as a clam, with a hard shell to match.'

I made no reply, but glanced over to his companion who had not stopped working. Following my gaze, Willet said: 'That's my son. We work together, casting small guns for merchantmen down at Bristol... falconets and such. They like to carry their own protection, against pirates.'

'Just the two of you?' I said. 'That must be hard work.'

He gave a shrug. 'It is, but I'd rather be my own man than serve the Mountfords as I used to.' A pause, then: 'Old Sir Richard was a good master, though we saw less of him after John took over...'

He looked away, but it was enough: I seized the moment.

29

'I know about the explosion,' I said. 'A terrible event... I heard Sir Richard was in anguish over his brother's death.'

The answer, however, astonished me. When Willett turned to face me again, he was frowning.

'Explosion?' He shook his head. 'Nay, there was none. John Mountford was found in the woods, crushed by a fallen tree.' And when I showed surprise: 'He too was a good man... I'm certain Crickepit would be a happier place, had he lived.'

Though eager to speak further, I held back; this was not the time, and he was eager to return to his work. I asked him if we might talk further in The Comfort that evening, when I would stand him a mug or two.

'You're a generous man, sir,' he said, after a pause. 'And most enquiring... I'll attend you, if you wish. Though I've no desire to speak of the Mountfords – I left their employ soon after Francis started coming here. Do you know him?'

I hesitated, then said that I may have met the man once. To which the foundryman gave a nod, and took his farewell.

But as he walked away, my pulse quickened. There had been no explosion: John Mountford had been killed by a falling tree. It was not unknown, I supposed, for a man to perish in such a manner – and yet, my Belstrang scepticism had possessed me.

In short, I did not believe it.

\*\*\*

That night at the inn was an unexpected turning point. It would send me further away than I expected, on a trail that would confound me. But I leap ahead in my account, and must tell of my conversation with Jonas Willett and his son, in a quiet corner of The Comfort Inn after supper.

I had not expected young Peter Willett to be there, but I was not displeased. Though at first somewhat guarded, after a while he began to speak with pride of his gun-founding. I was soon being overwhelmed with descriptions of small cannons:

30

minions, which threw a ball of four pounds; falcons, which are three-pounders, and falconets, two-pounders. They were nimble shipboard weapons, cast in good iron, Peter said. The Willetts, it transpired, had no license from the King to supply his army with ordnance. That was the Mountfords' business, at Crickepit and at their other foundries like Soudley, deeper in the forest.

'We don't have the means to make bigger cannon,' the older Willett said. 'Culverins, say, with a bore that can take an eighteen-pound shot. Or even demi-culverins. I learned my trade casting those… great heavy things.'

'I would be interested to watch the process,' I said, though in truth I was eager to turn to the topic of John Mountford's death. But I let the conversation flow for a while, plying both father and son with ale until I felt their tongues had loosened enough. The inn was almost full this night, the next day being the Sabbath; the talk was loud, with here and there voices rising in song.

'It's a dirty business, gun-founding… hot and perilous,' Jonas Willett said, before lapsing into silence. It struck me that he was the sort who might grow morose in drink, hence I sought to steer the discourse elsewhere.

'How do you ship them?' I enquired. 'By barge, downriver?'

'On trows,' Peter answered. 'Flat-bottomed sailing boats – you will see them up and down the Severn.'

I might have told him that I was as familiar with Severn trows as he was, since they sailed as far up the river as Worcester and even further – until I remembered that William Pride was supposed to be a Londoner.

'There's a pill – that's what we call creeks here on the Severn. It flows down to Purton on the riverfront,' Peter went on. 'That's where they dock, and we load our gunnery. Mountfords do the same… they have their own boats.'

'I believe I've heard that,' I said, my mind moving quickly.

'It was on such a boat that John Mountford's corpse was sent upriver, to their estate at Upton – am I correct?'

But to that, neither man spoke. They exchanged looks, and lifted their mugs.

'Your pardon...' I looked from one to the other. 'I recall it's not a matter you like to discuss.'

'My father has small liking for Francis Mountford – that's Sir Richard's son,' Peter said finally. 'But John was respected hereabouts... he is greatly missed.'

I glanced at the older man, but he had lapsed into silence.

'Is Francis here often?' I asked. 'For I recall that yesternight you spoke of men not being paid...'

'Him and Tobias Russell... a pair of thieves, if you ask me,' Jonas Willett grunted. 'I'll wager the old man don't know the half of what goes on down here.'

He was growing surly, taking longer pulls from his mug. Fearing that further refills of the Comfort's strong ale would prove unproductive, I addressed Peter.

'Will you say more?' I asked him. 'If we're to invest in mines and foundries here, my fellows and I need to learn all we can. It could be that we might offer employment in the future, for hard-working men.'

That last remark was careless, of course, and it shames me now to think of the deception I practised. But I thought of Richard Mountford on his sick-bed... his anxious face - and knew I must press home every opportunity.

'In truth, there's not a lot more to say, sir.' Peter was looking askance at me now. The old man, however, chimed in.

'Francis Mountford's a hard man... a true ironmaster,' he muttered. 'He rarely shows his face at Cricklepit, save when a large shipment's being readied. You might ask down at Purton wharf... when he's here, he spends more time there than he does at his foundries.' He gave a snort, then lapsed into silence.

'Well, perhaps I will,' I replied. I saw that Jonas's eyes were down, gazing at his scarred boots; I would learn nothing further. I lifted my mug and drained it, then feigned a yawn.

'I've enjoyed your company,' I said. 'But I'm away to my bed now. Perhaps we'll talk again?'

Peter rose, with a wary eye on his father. 'We do thank you for the ale, sir,' he said, somewhat formally. 'Now I'd best get us both home to our beds.'

He offered his hand, which I shook. Then I left them, making my way to the stairs. As I climbed, I looked back to see the young man bent over his sire, who was now dozing off.

\*\*\*

On the Sabbath morning I rose to the sound of a bell tolling from St Mary's, Lydney's parish church, where almost the entire village congregated. Meanwhile William Pride took a breakfast of porridge, bacon and small beer at the inn, before venturing forth to attend to his horse. Finding Leucippus well-cared for, I tipped the stable-boy to saddle him and bring him outdoors, then got myself mounted.

It was a short ride to Purton, along a well-used track. Soon I was beside the Severn again, though it was a very different river from the one familiar to me at Worcester: perhaps a mile wide, with the far bank barely visible. I drew rein, my eyes settling on the timbered wharf with its stacked cargo, square shapes covered with sailcloth. Moored to the dock was a fine sailing trow, its hold open and empty, no doubt ready for loading on the morrow. There was no-one in sight.

Dismounting, I left Leucippus and walked to the waterside to look at the boat: the name *Lady Ann* was painted on her prow. As I stood, a figure appeared abruptly from beneath the aft decking. I gave him good morning, but received no reply.

'A fine vessel,' I called out. 'Are you the master?'

My answer was a brief nod; the captain of the *Lady Ann*, I

would learn, was not a courteous man. But he walked to the landing-plank, stepped on to it and came ashore.

'Are you the new fellow?' He asked bluntly. He was perhaps forty years old, thin and scrawny, wearing a seaman's toque. 'I didn't expect you till tomorrow.'

'In truth, I regret I'm not the one you expected,' I answered. 'Just a man of business, poking about.'

A look of impatience appeared. 'I'd advise against that, sir,' the trow-master said. He turned away, but I stayed him.

'I'm a friend of the Mountfords, who's looking to invest hereabouts. Perhaps you and I might do business one day.'

He stopped to look me over, noting my sword in its scabbard. Finally, he asked which of the Mountfords I knew: would that be Francis, or his father? On impulse, I thought it wise to say it was Francis.

'I mistook you for another,' he muttered. 'I'll leave you to your walk.'

'Are those Mountford's cannons?' I asked, nodding towards the covered cargo. 'I suppose they're bound for Bristol?'

But the man was suspicious. 'I won't speak of that,' he answered. Again he made to move off, but I was eager to press what I believed was my advantage.

'My name's Pride,' I told him. 'I have iron works in the Kent Weald. Might I know your name?'

'It's Spry,' came the terse reply – at which a memory sprang up at once.

'Why, you're the man who took John Mountford's body upriver, to his father's house,' I said. 'I heard of it in Upton… such a sad and terrible accident.'

But if I had seen this as an opening, I was thwarted. Captain Spry clammed up, turned from me and stepped swiftly away. I watched him walk up the gangplank on to his vessel, and disappear under the awning.

In doing so, however, the man had erred. For his very actions had aroused the suspicions of ex-Justice Belstrang – had they not existed already. Something was being hidden from me, and I intended to find out what.

I would return the next day, I resolved, to watch *The Lady Ann* being loaded – and no-one was going to prevent me.

\*\*\*

That night at The Comfort I took supper alone, intending to retire early; as was my habit, I would gather my thoughts and begin compiling a report of what I had learned. But when I asked Henry Hawes for ink and paper, the landlord spread his hands sadly. There was none to be had just now, I was told… did I wish to send a letter?

It was of no import, I replied; a trifling matter. But I watched him walk off, and unease settled upon me: I felt certain the man was lying.

My mind busy, I sat in the same corner where I had spoken with the Willetts, neither of whom was present that night. I decided to put aside William Pride's initial bonhomie and assume the appearance of a man with matters on his mind, who did not wish to be troubled - which indeed, was true enough. But a short while later, as I finished my mug and was about to go, an incident occurred which would change everything.

The first I knew of it was a raising of voices, and a scraping of stools as someone got quickly to their feet. Sensing that a scuffle was about to break out, I stood up, peering over the heads of drinkers. Others were doing the same, a general hubbub rising. I looked about, but Hawes the landlord was nowhere to be seen. Whereupon, having no wish to be a party or even witness to a brawl, I started towards the staircase – but I was too late. Without warning two men careered towards me, locked in a tussle, and almost threw me off my balance. Others followed, cursing and shouting.

In consternation I fell back, reaching instinctively for my sword as the two combatants fell to the floor, rolling and punching. But instead of leaving them to settle their differences, the entire company appeared bent on giving one of the men a beating, gathering to deliver curses and kicks.

For Justice Belstrang, of course, this was too much.

'Enough!' I shouted, drawing my old rapier and raising it. 'Stand aside, or I'll cut the next man who strikes a blow!'

To my relief, the assault ceased as heads turned towards me; mercifully, my authority seemed to be sufficient. Men stepped back, leaving the two tusslers on the floor, one atop the other. This one turned quickly to glare at me.

''Tis none of your affair,' he snapped. 'Get away!'

'I won't,' I returned, looking down at his victim, who was already blooded. 'Cease your brabble, or I'll-'

'You will not, Master Pride,' said a voice close by.

I looked round to see Henry Hawes, an oak billet in his hand, shouldering his way forward in determined fashion. It seemed he was no stranger to disturbances, and at his approach The Comfort's customers moved away.

'I'll take care of this, sir,' he said. 'If you'll be good enough to withdraw.'

'Gladly,' I breathed, lowering my sword. Thereafter I watched as Hawes seized the man whom I now believed was the chief troublemaker by the arm, and dragged him aside.

'He's had enough,' he said, looking at the one on the floor, who was the slighter of the two. 'So have you, Combes – enough to drink, that is. Go home and sleep it off.'

There was a moment's silence, but it was over. With a scowl the heavier man got up, massaging his bruised knuckles. Without a word he pushed his way through the watchers and made for the door. All eyes were now on the bloodied figure who sat up, panting, and peered blearily about him.

'Can you stand, Peck?' Henry Hawes was saying. He looked round. 'Will someone lend a hand, to help me lift him?'

But nobody came forward. Instead men were turning away, returning to their seats. Some headed for the door.

'I will do so,' I said. Having sheathed my sword, I stepped to the landlord's side, ready to offer a hand – whereupon to my surprise, the loser of the fight scowled.

'I need no help from anyone!' He cried. 'You Cricklepit men – a curse on the whole pack of you!'

I gazed at him: a grizzled fellow clad in dusty green. But as his eyes focussed on me, his expression changed: I was not one of the Cricklepit men. Lowering his gaze, he put hands to the floor and heaved himself to his feet, grunting with pain.

'You know better than to pick a fight here, Peck,' Henry Hawes said, relieved to see that the man could stand up.

'I didn't seek it,' Master Peck retorted. He put a hand to his mouth and inspected the blood upon it. Raising his gaze suddenly, he looked about.

'You foundry bastards,' he cried, 'you'll be the ruin of this forest! Cutting trees down like they were corn, for your whoreson furnaces - soon there'll be nothing left! You varlets who serve that rogue Mountford – I curse every one of you!'

There was angry muttering at that, and one or two men looked as if they would act, but Hawes was having none of it.

'You're leaving,' he said to Peck. 'Get yourself home, and forbear to come here for a while.' He put a hand on the beaten man's shoulder and began to shove him – whereupon Peck staggered, putting a hand to his forehead.

'Let me help,' I said.

Hawes paused, then gave a nod. The two of us, one at either shoulder, steered the man to the door and out into the night air. There he stood, breathing hard, as with a last glance the landlord turned and went back inside. A moment passed, while Peck surveyed me with a puzzled look.

'Why did you aid me?' He asked. 'Are you not one of them?'

'Let me accompany you homeward,' I said, with a glance at the inn. 'For it strikes me you might not get far before someone in there comes out after you – and this time, you won't get up.'

And when the other hesitated, I took a chance.

'Besides,' I told him, 'I'm interested to hear about the rogue Mountford. Perhaps you and I may have something in common. Shall we walk?'

# FIVE

He was from the tiny hamlet of Aylburton, no more than a mile away: a forester, whose family had been here for generations. Long before the iron men came, he said; that started in the time of King Henry the Eighth. Why? Because iron cannon cost only a third of what bronze ones cost – did I not know that?

I told him that I had heard so, but said nothing about having an interest in mining, let alone cannons. Instead, as we walked the lane by moonlight, I asked him about the Mountfords. Was Francis Mountford the rogue, I asked? Or did he mean the man's uncle, the late John Mountford?

But Master Peck grew wary, and I feared he would prove reticent. Well, John Mountford had been a fair man, he allowed, even if he was as much to blame as others were for tearing up the forest. As for Francis... he drew a breath.

'I'd not tangle with that one,' he muttered. 'Cold-hearted, like his foundry-master.'

'I know Tobias Russell,' I said, to encourage him. 'Guards Cricklepit like a fortress... I'd not tangle with him, either.'

'May I ask what your interest is here, master?' Peck said then. He stopped, squinting at me in the dim light; it was time for some invention.

'I prefer not to answer that,' I said, after a pause. 'But I will say it's justice that drives me, not desire for wealth. And I've no more liking for Master Francis than you have.'

The other said nothing, but resumed walking stiffly. Falling in beside him, I sought for some further words to draw him out, when to my surprise he said: 'You're not the first to come here asking questions. There was a man a year or so back, turned out to be an agent of Spain, working for the Papists. He was took by some soldiers, in the end.'

'Well, I assure you I'm not one of that party,' I said, somewhat sharply. 'On the contrary…'

I broke off, berating myself. From being William Pride the investor, was I now about to pose as an agent of the Crown? I was beginning to find the deception game somewhat trying. Fortunately, Master Peck was barely listening. Instead, his eyes strayed upwards, to the heavens.

'Do you see that?' He said, pointing. 'The Great Comet – she's there every night' And when I nodded: 'Some are saying it's a bad omen.'

'So I've heard,' I replied. Whereupon Peck lowered his gaze, and drew a breath. 'There are things hereabouts you wouldn't want to delve into too deeply here, master,' he murmured. 'Then, when riches are to be gained, when was it not so?' With that, he stopped again and turned to face me.

'I thank you for aiding me,' he said. 'But I'll walk alone now. You'll want to be getting back.'

'Stay a moment,' I said. I believed I was on the verge of learning something of value, which might slip away. 'I'll admit one thing to you: that I serve the King's peace, and no other. If you can tell me anything about the Mountfords that they would prefer I didn't know, I'll be in your debt.'

For a while Peck regarded me with a frown, so that I fully expected him to turn away. But to my surprise, he answered.

'You might ask about the Concord Men,' he said, speaking low. 'But be most careful… that's all I will say.'

And he was gone, walking heavily.

I watched him disappear into the gloom, before turning round to return to Lydney. So deep in thought was I, I failed to hear the footsteps until it was too late – until a shape loomed out of nowhere, causing me to stop in my tracks. Then something whirled through the air, and there came a crack on my skull that stunned me. As I staggered, half-dazed, a voice close to my ear

40

hissed a warning that I barely made out, though later I would recall it plainly enough:

'Leave and return whence you came - or next time the blow will be fatal.'

After that there was only a sound of heavy boots, hurrying away into the dark. And yet, as the warning voice still rang in my head, I knew I had heard it before; when and where, however, I could not tell.

\*\*\*

The next morning. I awoke in my chamber at The Comfort with an aching head, a dry mouth and a powerful thirst for revenge. And quickly, the events of the previous night came into focus.

I recalled returning to the inn, and entering to a sudden silence. Men had paused at their drinking, mugs half-way to mouths, regarding me without expression. My head throbbed from the blow I had received, but thankfully there was no blood. Shaken, but striving to appear unconcerned, I made my way to the staircase as Henry Hawes appeared, a look of apparent concern on his face.

'Are you all right, Master Pride?'

'Of course,' I answered at once. 'Why should I not be?'

'No matter, sir. Shall I send a mug up to your chamber, or-'

'No,' I broke in. 'I'm weary, and will go to my bed.' I met his eye, then glanced round to find men still gazing at me.

'In fact,' I added, 'I'm weary of the company here, too. Mayhap I'll seek accommodation elsewhere - good-night.'

Now, as the words came back to me, I sat up and regretted not accepting the drink. The morning was already advanced, I saw, sunlight streaming in. With an effort I rose and shuffled to the window – then I remembered that it was Monday, and I had intended to ride down to Purton again to watch cannons being loaded.

I threw the casement wide and drew some breaths, then took my time dressing, feeling a lump on my head the size of a plover's egg. I was angry – as much at my own carelessness as for the stark warning I had received. I would never be able to identify my assailant, for I had barely seen him, though I believed he had come from the inn. If I were to remain here, I knew I would be in danger. As for finding accommodation elsewhere, that could be difficult: The Comfort was the only inn for miles.

I took a light breakfast without leaving my room; nor did the wench who brought it address a word to me. I had barely noticed her before, but supposed she was Hawes's daughter. Presently I descended and ventured outdoors, without seeing the landlord. I took Leucippus from the stables and saddled him myself, glad to be out in morning sunshine. Then I was in the saddle, riding down to Purton where the cries of gulls greeted me. And now a very different sight appeared: the wharf was bustling with activity.

I dismounted and strode casually to the quay, where as I had expected the *Lady Ann* was being loaded. A small crane was at work, creaking on its swivel as men swung it from the dock to the vessel, where others waited to unfasten its burden. One glance was enough: the cargo was indeed the barrel of a large cannon, its muzzle stuffed with wadding. Glancing at the wharf, I saw the neat stacks of cannon-trunks uncovered and ready for loading.

Soon a figure drew near, whereupon I turned to find myself facing none other than Captain Spry once again. I gave him good morning, but this time there was no vestige of courtesy; in short, the man was belligerence personified.

'What do you want here?' He demanded. 'You're in the way of our lading, and the tide won't wait.'

'I'll keep back,' I replied, my face free of expression. 'I

42

wouldn't want to delay you.'

'The work is private – King's business,' Spry grunted.

'I told you who I am, yesterday,' I said. 'You ship the Mountfords' ordnance downriver, and unload at Bristol. From there I assume it's taken round the coast to London, then up the Thames to the Tower, where anyone can see guns lying on the wharf. What's secret about it?'

'Well, if you know so much, why do you come to gawp?' The other threw back.

I tried to form an answer, aware that some of the wharfmen were looking our way. Behind them, the little crane continued to creak on its swivel. Once more, it was time for some invention.

'In truth, I have reason,' I said, thinking fast. 'Francis Mountford asked me to come here. Since his uncle's death, he suspects there are things he's not been told.' And when Spry's brow furrowed, I added: 'I'll be meeting him again soon… I'm sure he'd want you to offer me every assistance.'

'Like what?' Spry snapped. But he was uneasy, eyes moving to his vessel, which swayed at anchor.

I looked away, towards the three or four men who had been watching us. Spry saw them too, and jerked his head to suggest there was nothing amiss. But as they returned to their work one figure remained, and the next moment he was walking towards us. As he approached, I realised he was a foreigner: dark-complexioned, with a great black moustache and beard, clad in loose cotton clothing with an embroidered cap on his head. Drawing close to Spry, he gave him a questioning look but did not speak.

'It's naught,' Spry said, turning to him. 'A friend of my master… Pride, was that your name?' And when I gave a nod: 'He's come to look at the guns…'

'Good morning,' I broke in, facing the newcomer. 'Might I

know your name?'

The other gave no answer, merely stared.

'He's Yakup,' Spry said tersely. 'He sails with me... he doesn't have much English.'

He was impatient to go - too impatient, I thought. The man was torn between not wishing to insult a friend of the Mountford family, and an eagerness to be rid of me - but on a sudden, I experienced a feeling of liberation. Justice Belstrang might have had reservations, but William Pride had none. I saw a way forward – and a notion sprang up.

'Why, he's a Turk,' I said, glancing from Spry to Yakup and back. 'The name is Turkish, is it not?' And before the other could answer, I gestured to the man's broad leather belt, from which a silver charm dangled. 'That's the hand of Fatima, brings good fortune... I've seen it before, in London.'

'Mayhap you have,' Spry returned sourly. 'I ask not where a man hails from... he's a seafarer, that's all that matters to me.'

'A long way from home, though, is he not?'

I was calm now. I was certain that Spry knew this man was Turkish - and it was the first time I'd heard of anyone from the distant Sultanate working on a Severn trow. I raised my brows at the captain – but his patience was at an end.

'See now, I don't have time to stand and gossip,' he muttered. 'You may poke about, as you put it, the whole day if you wish. And you may tell Master Francis, when you see him, that I sailed on the afternoon tide with a full cargo. Now, with your leave...'

He put a hand on Yakup's shoulder, and the two walked off without looking back. Meanwhile, another cannon swung from the crane's jib on its way to the *Lady Ann's* hold... and my suspicions hardened.

Spry was hiding something, just as Tobias Russell had been hiding something. I had no notion what it was, but my course was clear: I would defy those who wished to dissuade me, and plough a straight furrow - wherever it led.

I walked back to Leucippus and, with a last glance at the wharf, got myself mounted and rode apace back to Lydney... where I heard tidings that confounded me.

The forester Thomas Peck, whom I had helped homewards the previous night, had been found dead.

\*\*\*

'Where was he found?'

I demanded this of Henry Hawes, the two of us standing in the inn, which was devoid of customers that morning. I had learned the news from him after enquiring about the man who came off worse in the brawl. Hawes was unwilling to speak of the matter, but saw that I was in no humour for evasion. With many a shake of his head, he replied that Peck appeared to have collapsed in the street at Aylburton, but a short way from his home, and cracked his head. He was unsteady on his feet, the landlord reminded me – I knew it as well as anyone, did I not? To my mind, he seemed most keen to stress that it had been an unfortunate mishap – an accident.

I stared at him, until he dropped his gaze.

'Two days ago,' I said. 'I learned of a man being killed by a falling tree. Now I hear of another who fell over in the street - even though he was walking well enough when I last saw him.' In growing anger, I raised a hand and pointed. 'There appear to have been a troubling number of fatal accidents hereabouts, wouldn't you say?'

Hawes merely shrugged.

'Moreover,' I added, 'someone caught me on the road last night and gave me a blow to the head, soon after I'd bidden Peck goodnight. I wonder if the same thing happened to him?'

'I don't follow you, sir.' A blank look had come over the landlord's face, similar to the one I had seen on Tobias Russell.

Its meaning was plain: I would learn nothing further.

I turned away to go up to my chamber, but stopped, seething with anger; something was gravely amiss here, and I wanted answers. On impulse, I walked to the door and went out.

Within a short time, I was riding Leucippus up the Lyd to the Cricklepit foundry, where I drew rein and waited.

The place was as noisy as before, with smoke issuing from the furnace chimney. I remained in the saddle, until soon enough the man I wanted to see appeared in his leather apron, wearing an expression of disapproval.

'Master Pride...' Russell came within a few yards, then halted. 'Here you are again.'

'So I am,' I said. 'I've been busy since we last met, talking to people. I spent an interesting hour at Purton earlier, with Captain Spry. He was most forthcoming.'

Russell made no reply, but shifted his stance slightly.

'I met one of his crewmen, a Turk,' I went on. 'Curious...'

'What is it you want of me?' The other broke in. 'I've no time to spare in idle chatter.'

'Those were Spry's very words, too,' I said brightly. 'Before I reassured him of my intentions, that is.'

I was thinking hard, trying to construct some means of penetrating the man's exterior... *tight as a clam*, Jonas Willett had said. I met his eye, but discerned nothing.

'What intentions?' Russell demanded. 'You said you were-'

'I said I was interested in cannons,' I broke in. 'That's your trade, is it not?'

'You know that already,' the other returned.

'Indeed – ordnance for the King,' I said. 'But I wonder now if all of your guns go to His Majesty... might some of them find their way elsewhere?'

Well, I must confess it: I have no idea where that notion sprang from. Likely it had been taking shape in my mind since

I talked with the Willetts, and with Spry... but finding Yakup the Turk in his company must have crystallised it. I pictured that man again, and suspected that he was no sailor. His manner of dress, the way he had walked up to Spry with that questioning look... William Pride was on unsteady ground, but he would hold it. And to my relief the strategy worked – though it did not seem so at first.

'What do you mean?'

For the first time, Russell showed emotion. Taking a sudden step forward, he made as if to grasp Leucippus's bridle - but in that he erred badly. The horse jerked his head, veering away from the man, and bared his teeth. At once I got down from the saddle, took the bridle myself and murmured a few words. As Leucippus calmed, I turned to face the other, whose anger was now plain.

'I know something's in train here,' I said, giving my voice an edge. 'And I think I know what it is. But you're not a fool. Do you not see that it could be to your advantage?'

There was a brief silence. From the corner of my eye, I saw foundrymen gathering as before, watching alertly. Things could turn ugly, and before I knew it my hand was on my sword-hilt.

'What advantage?'

Russell's manner had changed. He was still hostile, but there was a look in his eye that I knew well enough: one of pure greed. Seizing the moment, I pressed it home.

'I told you, I have customers of my own,' I said, lowering my voice. 'Men who pay well, and who keep their mouths shut.'

'So, all you said about foundries and investing and such, was a pack of lies,' the other replied, with a sneering look.

I remained silent, but took my hand from my sword.

'Now you come here, bold as brass, and think I'd do business with you at the drop of a coin,' he went on. 'A man I know little of, and would trust even less?'

'I don't trust you either, Russell,' I said. 'But I'll live with it.'

Another silence followed. But the foundry-master glanced round at his men, and made a dismissive gesture. As they moved away, he faced me and lifted a calloused hand.

'I might hear you out,' he said, pointing at me. 'But you should know the risks. Nobody thwarts me – no-one.'

I met his eye, and saw that it was no bluff - and on a sudden, a chill swept over me. John Mountford... had he thwarted this man, and paid the price? Had he learned of underhand dealings, and intended to take action? Justice Belstrang would have demanded an answer – but William Pride saw which way the wind blew, and made his decision.

'Understood,' I said, letting out a breath. 'Now shall we go somewhere private, and talk of culverins and demi-culverins? Or shall we talk first of money?'

## SIX

Well now, here is the plain truth I learned that day from Tobias Russell: that unbeknown to Sir Richard Mountford, and no doubt unbeknown to King James too, the Cricklepit foundry was quietly shipping cannons to the Great Turk.

At first, I could barely compass what I heard. But I listened intently, hiding my feelings. Sultan Osman the Second, it seemed, had usurped his uncle a while back and was eager to strengthen his position. English guns were prized throughout Europe and beyond... and naturally, there was money to be made.

'So... the man Yakup,' I said finally, still struggling to grasp the matter. 'Is he there to oversee shipments?'

Russell gave a shrug. The two of us sat in a small, cluttered room close to the furnace-house, where the smell of burning charcoal was strong. 'It's a long voyage from Bristol to Constantinople,' he murmured. 'The Sultan don't trust Englishmen to keep a bargain, though we trade all the time.'

'Surely the whole of your cargo doesn't go there? I asked. 'It would be too obvious-'

'Of course it doesn't,' Russell growled. 'The dividing is done at Bristol...' he was frowning. 'I think I've told you enough. Let's hear what you have to say – your proposition.'

I tried to assume a hard look. 'It's simple enough. How many can you supply, and what's your price?'

I waited, making an effort to control my shock at what I had stumbled upon. Now I seemed to have become a dealer in armaments – or William Pride had. Perhaps I should adopt a more brutal manner, I thought: Russell was suspicious of me, and would remain so. It sobered me to think what Sir Richard Mountford would think, if he knew where some of his cannons ended up. As for the King... my pulse quickened. Surely what

Russell did could amount to treason?

Then something sprang to mind: the last words I had heard from Thomas Peck... perhaps the last words, I realised, that he had ever spoken. 'The Concord Men,' I said. 'Are they the ones who have set this trade in motion?'

But I had missed my mark: in a moment Russell's gamester's face was back.

'Who?' He enquired.

'No matter...' I looked away, cursing inwardly. 'I'll forget I heard the words.'

He eyed me, and for a moment I feared he would refuse to proceed any further. I had touched a nerve: the Concord Men, whoever they were, would have to wait.

'Given time, I could supply twenty culverins,' he said, in a bland voice. 'To be mounted on carriages, at buyer's will. Long-barrelled ones, if they're for ships. Iron cannonballs too, eighteen pounders.'

The man's directness was unexpected. Gathering my wits, I pretended to consider.

'How many shipments are we talking about?'

'It depends how many you want. Five cannon trunks can be diverted on the quays at Bristol at one time, for transfer to another vessel. That's yours to arrange – my part of the business ends as soon as they're unloaded from the trow.'

'That's four river voyages,' I objected. 'The goods would need to be stored, until the whole consignment had arrived.'

'Again, that's your affair,' Russell replied tersely. 'It's not a trade for the witless - or the faint-hearted. And I don't want to know who your buyers are, any more than you need concern yourself with mine.'

'I know that,' I said, putting on a frown. 'Mayhap it's time we spoke of prices.'

At that, Russell relaxed. Whether he had decided I was a *bona fide* arms trader, or was merely relishing the prospect of a lucrative payment, I did not know... but on a sudden, I was uneasy: in truth, I realised, I had not the least idea what an iron-cast cannon should cost.

The matter was compounded when he gave another shrug and said: 'Why don't you make me an offer?'

I lowered my gaze, fumbling for an answer... whereupon a solution occurred, which brought a mixture of hope and alarm. It was rash, perhaps, but it seemed the best way forward, if not the only way. Drawing a breath, I looked up.

'I want to see for myself how the shipments are handled between here and Bristol, and then at the port.'

'Why?' Russell demanded at once. 'How the goods reach Bristol is already known to you. You only need take delivery.'

'Nevertheless, I want assurance,' I persisted. And when he continued to look displeased: 'It's a large investment. My fellows would want a report before committing themselves.'

'You haven't yet said how much you're willing to pay,' the other replied.

'No, I haven't,' I agreed. 'But I say this: let me sail downriver with Spry on the *Lady Ann*, and observe what happens at Bristol. If I think all is safe and watertight, I'll return here and agree a price, with a sum paid in advance.' On impulse, I added: 'If I'm satisfied, there'll be a purse for yourself, that won't appear on the reckoning.'

For a while Russell eyed me with evident mistrust; I could almost hear him calculating. It was a taut moment, until to my relief, he let out a sigh and nodded.

'Very well, if it will set your mind at ease.'

He stood up, glancing towards the half-open door. 'I'll give you a note for Spry, telling him to take you to Bristol and back.' With a thin smile, he added: 'There's no comfort to be had... you'll sleep alongside the crew. The Turk, too... and I'd keep a wary eye on that one.'

I said nothing, merely rose and went out into the foundry yard. Standing by Leucippus, breathing somewhat hard, I waited until Russell appeared with a paper folded into a tight square, tied with cord. But as I reached out to take it, he grasped my hand tightly.

'Now I'll say this, Pride,' he breathed, leaning close. 'If you ever let slip one word of what I've told you, your life will be ended. You may be certain of that.'

In silence I met his gaze. My impulse was to ask if he was the one who had sent someone to deliver that painful warning, two days earlier. But I merely waited for him to let go, took the paper and got myself mounted.

As I rode away, I glanced back to see the man watching me – and even from a distance I saw his look of unallayed menace. Urging the horse to a canter, I strove to put thoughts of Master Russell from my mind, and faced up to what lay ahead.

I could only hope I was in time to catch the afternoon tide.

\*\*\*

The next hours passed in a hurry.

Back at The Comfort, I sought out Hawes and told him that I would be away for a while, and was obliged to leave Leucippus in his stable. As I handed money over, I held his gaze and let him understand that if anything was amiss when I returned, the consequences would be grave: the horse was precious to me, and should have only the best of care. In addition, I gave him a small sum to keep my chamber for my return. He listened until our business was concluded, then:

'Do you intend to walk, Master Pride? There's naught but forest in every direction... save the river, of course.'

I met his eye, but read nothing. Not for the first time, I suspected this man knew more than he told - but I was in a hurry. 'I'll return in a few days,' I said brusquely. Whereupon I made haste to go up to my room and gather my belongings. There was little to pack, of course: what had started out as a brief journey four days before, to stay overnight with Sir Richard at Foxhill, had turned into something quite different.

Soon I was outside again, walking as quickly as I could along the track to Purton. Time was short, the afternoon was advancing and I'd had no dinner. Russell's words came back to me as I walked: I expected little hospitality from Captain Spry, and an uncomfortable voyage ahead. I was unsure how far it was, downriver to Bristol... twenty miles? Setting my jaw tight, I forged ahead in the sunshine, perspiring as I went.

Mercifully I was in time, but only just.

The wharf was quiet. One or two men stood about, but the crane was idle, the stack of cannon-trunks gone. The *Lady Ann,* fully laden, sat low in the water, her cargo covered with sheeting. No sails were raised, but doubtless she would embark soon... I made my way to the trow's side, then saw to my dismay that there was no gangplank.

Feeling mighty conspicuous, if not foolish, I called out. After a moment one of the crewmen appeared, to be joined by another. With some gesturing, I made them understand that I was a passenger, with authorisation for the captain. I held up the paper and waited, until at last Spry emerged from behind the aft awning. I watched him confer with his men, then look my way... whereupon his curse was plainly audible, and as vile as only a sailor's curses can be.

But still I waited, my unease growing until I half-expected the man to set sail without me. Hence my relief was great when the gangplank was brought from somewhere and thrown across the gap between quayside and vessel. Without further delay I hoisted my pack of belongings and clambered aboard, proffering my paper before me. Spry snatched it, tore it open and read the scrawled message with a face of thunder. Then he faced me, and spoke up.

'Lord help me, Pride, but the moment you give me the least cause, I'll let you fall over the side – you and your whoreson letter of passage. But first I'll wait until we're on a fast current, so you're swept out into the Channel... if you don't drown, the sharks will have you. Do you understand me?'

To which I drew a long breath, tamped down Justice Belstrang's indignation, and forced a nod.

And within a quarter hour all was bustle aboard the trow, as the mast was raised from where it had lain on her deck: the customary position, to enable her to pass under bridges. Her sails were hoisted, then as the wind filled them, ropes were thrown from the quayside. And soon after that we were moving south-west on the broad river, with the afternoon sun ahead.

\*\*\*

That night I slept beneath the stars; there was no room under the aft decking where Spry, his three crewmen and Yakup lay, packed together and bundled in blankets. There had been no disagreement: once the captain showed me how small was the space, I had volunteered. The night was not too cold – and there was the imposing sight of the Great Comet, fiery-tailed, still bright in the southern sky. I thought briefly of home, of Hester and Childers with his warnings of doom, before managing to sleep a little. This was despite the rocking at anchor of the Lady Ann, the snores from the rear, and the fact that I had eaten nothing but bread and cheese, shared grudgingly with me by Spry's crewmen. That, and the grim feeling that I could be on a wasted journey.

For I was unsure now that I would learn anything from watching the trow unload her cargo; Russell's readiness to let me observe the business was testimony to that. Mulling over the matter, I eventually drifted off to sleep, to be rudely awoken by the captain bawling at his men. I stirred, stiff and uncomfortable in the morning chill, and discovered that we were shrouded in mist.

Thereafter, it was a long day. The distance, I learned, was approximately seven leagues; Spry did not expect to reach the Bristol quays until nightfall. He was ill-tempered and mostly ignored me, but I will admit he was a good sailor whose men obeyed him without question. Sitting stiffly on top of the cargo, moving only rarely to stretch my legs and trying to keep out of the way, I watched the distant banks pass by and held my peace... and eventually found my eyes on Yakup the Turk, who never spoke. There was something unsettling about the man, I decided, especially given the long knife he carried at his belt. Finally he caught my eye, and a look of such brazen hostility appeared that I turned away.

By mid-day the mist had lifted, and the voyage passed without incident. We saw many vessels on the widening estuary, and were forced to tack when the wind changed, but as the sun was setting the *Lady Ann* made a sweep to port, and quite soon we had left the Severn and were sailing up the River Avon into Bristol. Finally Spry brought his vessel into the crowded harbour, sails were lowered and we drew alongside Broad Quay. Ropes were thrown, sailors and wharfmen exchanged shouts, and the trow was still, heaving gently at her moorings.

And Robert Belstrang, alias William Pride, stumbled ashore with a grumbling stomach, stiff legs and a feeling of relief. I am no seafarer, and resolved there and then that I would remain on land for the rest of my life... except that there was a return journey yet to be made.

Night was drawing in, and lanterns were being lit about the harbourside. I took my leave of Spry, who barely grunted a reply. When I asked about the unloading, I was told that it would likely take all of the following day, and he intended to set sail the morning after that, at first light. Having said all he would, he left me to my own devices and stalked off.

Hence, I need not dwell upon my immense satisfaction at finding a bright-lit tavern close by, where I could eat and drink to my heart's content and, for a while at least, put aside the wearisome guise of William Pride, unscrupulous dealer in weaponry.

***

I slept late at the inn I had found, a few streets away from the harbour. The place was busy, but I was able to bespeak a stay of one further night. Having taken breakfast, I ventured out into the teeming streets and made my way down to the quayside. There were several large vessels in port, which I observed with interest. With so many people about – wharfmen and sailors, porters and tradesmen as well as a sprinkling of idlers and drabs – few paid much attention to me as I wandered among them, finally arriving beside the *Lady Ann* once again. Here I was surprised to see not only Spry and his crewmen, but two soldiers in royal livery, standing on the quay. Before they observed me, I thought it best to withdraw; I had no desire to answer questions. As I moved away, a reason for their presence occurred: this was, supposedly at least, a consignment of ordnance bound for the Royal Armouries. Likely the soldiers were to provide an escort, to see that it reached its destination safely.

Whereupon a notion made me stop in my tracks: the dividing of the cargo was done here, Russell had said. How, I wondered, was this carried out under the noses of the King's guards?

I moved some distance away, and found a convenient station behind a stack of bales; there was no shortage of cover on the cluttered quayside. From here, I began to watch the unloading. In fact it had begun hours ago: there was a crane in position, lowering its hook to the deck of the trow. As Spry's men attached ropes, I saw that several cannons had already been

56

hefted ashore and were lying on the quay.

I set myself to wait.

An hour passed, then two; the sun was high, and I grew bored and restless. Two neat stacks of cannon now stood on the quay, one smaller than the other. Already the *Lady Ann* sat higher in the water, but I guessed that the hold was not even half-emptied. Stiffly I moved away from my vantage point and, perhaps somewhat incautiously, ventured closer to the vessel. I saw the crewmen at work, but there was no sign of Spry... whereupon I halted: there was no sign of the soldiers either. It was past noon... had they gone off somewhere to take dinner? Why would they leave their posts?

On a sudden, my attention was caught by the actions of three rough-clad porters, standing by one of the stacks of ordnance. There was a flat, low-sided barrow nearby, and these brawny fellows were lifting one cannon-trunk high enough to rest it there. I was curious: was this the usual practice? I had a notion that cargo was generally transferred by lighters from a small vessel to a larger ship, as I had seen on the Thames in London... but as I have said, my knowledge of such matters is limited. So I watched from a discreet distance until three cannons had been placed on the truckle, which appeared to be as much as the porters would manage. A piece of sailcloth was thrown over the load, and at once two of them gripped the handles and set off.

Whereupon, I realised, my best course was to follow them and see where they ended up. It transpired that it was the right decision, by which I came to understood what was being done, here in a busy harbour in broad daylight.

Looking about them, the men set off through the throng, calling for people to make way. I followed as they weaved between obstacles, bales and stacks of timber. Finally, having passed two smaller vessels, they came to a halt alongside a good-sized merchantman, her foredeck towering above the quayside. A broad gangplank with a handrail sloped from the vessel's high side down to the ground, and one of the porters hastened up it to where two seamen stood. While they conferred briefly, I made my way idly to the stern of the ship, and saw her name painted in red lettering: *Waarheid.*

I would recall later that the word meant *truth*, but it was of small consequence, for I knew what language that was: the ship was Dutch. And I was non-plussed: was this Dutch merchantman bound for London and the Royal Armouries - or was she bound for the Mediterranean, and thence for far-off Constantinople, and the armouries of the Great Turk?

I did not attempt to find out. Instead I turned and made my way back to where the *Lady Ann* was moored. I would go aboard, accost Captain Spry and try to squeeze a few answers from him – whether he was willing or not.

## SEVEN

As usual the captain was morose, and I was obliged to remind him that I did business with Tobias Russell... private business, I added. Yet it failed to impress the man; he was not only bad-tempered that morning, but taut and preoccupied, his eyes straying often to the cannons as, one by one, they were raised laboriously from his hold and lowered to the quay.

'I've no time for this, Pride,' he snapped. 'Return tomorrow morning, and I'll take you back to Lydney as I was ordered. Then you and I are done.'

'What's happened to the guards?' I asked. 'Are they at dinner?'

He made no answer, only looked away. But knowing I should be bold as William Pride should be, I pressed on.

'Do the Mountfords always use Dutch vessels? I couldn't help but see where some of your cargo went.'

There was a moment then, before Spry turned somewhat slowly to face me – and now, there was not merely suspicion in his gaze: there was alarm.

'What in God's name is that to you?'

'It's my business to know such things,' I returned. 'Did Russell not tell you, in his letter?'

'He did not.'

'Well, no matter...' I put on a look of unconcern. 'It's of no consequence to me who carries your goods, so long as they arrive safely.' With that, I allowed my gaze to stray to the quayside. The two porters had not yet returned with their barrow, but the third man had thrown a covering over the smaller stack of cannon, and was now seated upon it. Facing Spry again, I feigned a yawn.

'Where's your friend, the Turk?' I enquired. 'I expected him to be out here, watching.'

But this time, my answer was sharp. Without warning, Spry's hand shot up to grasp the collar of my shirt.

'What game do you play?' His voice was cracked as an old pot. 'Or mayhap I should ask, who sent you?'

'I've told you I'm a man of business, and my business is gunnery,' I returned, my heart making a jump. 'And if you don't let go of me, I'll...'

My hand was on my sword-hilt, the two of us almost touching. I smelled the man's sour breath, and put on as threatening a look as I could – whereupon there was a sudden noise from the rear of the vessel. Looking aside quickly, I saw two of Spry's crewmen appear from beneath the rear decking, throwing aside the sheet that served as a screen. With them were the two soldiers in royal livery... and one glance was enough: both guards were so drunk, they could barely stand.

But the tension was broken. At once Spry released me and stepped away, turning to his guests. Those two, I realised, had been plied with drink while part of the King's ordnance was being rolled away... so simply, and so brazenly. Breathing hard, I glanced from the captain to his crewmen, one of whom threw him a knowing smirk.

'I'll be back in the morning, for the return voyage,' I said to Spry. 'Then as you said, we're done.'

I moved swiftly to the gangplank and got myself ashore. As I walked away, I looked round to see the captain and his men helping the soldiers along the deck... and recalled that my earlier question had gone unanswered: where was Yakup?

But I dismissed the matter: doubtless he would leave England along with the Sultan's cannons. I assumed I would not see him again... but in that respect, I was gravely mistaken.

\*\*\*

I spent the remainder of the day in my chamber at the inn. I had called for pen, ink and paper which were brought at once –

which afforded me some relief, after Henry Hawes's refusal back at The Comfort. Now I could compose my report, which would help me put matters into focus. I began with my talk at the bedside of Richard Mountford, and detailed each subsequent day's events until I arrived at Bristol. Here I broke off to take a supper, before returning to add a few questions to my account, to whit:

How many people were aware of this dangerous trade Tobias Russell was engaged in? Was Francis Mountford steeped in it, up to his neck? Could he even have ordered his uncle's death, if John had uncovered what was going on? And finally, the question that had begun to gnaw at me:

Who were the Concord Men?

Alas, I had no answers; nor was I sure of my next move once I returned to Lydney. Setting aside my account, I went down to take supper before retiring early. I had packed my belongings, and asked the host to arouse me before dawn.

He did so, seemingly but minutes after I had fallen asleep. I rose quickly, dressed by candlelight, settled the reckoning and left the inn without taking breakfast, just as the city of Bristol was coming to life. Hurrying through the gloomy streets, I readied myself for a grim day's sailing, under the eye of a captain who was deeply suspicious of me. But I thrust the notion aside and reached the quayside where men were already about, with the cries of gulls overhead. I approached Spry's mooring, squinting ahead... then stopped in my tracks.

There was no sign of the *Lady Ann* – only an empty space at the waterside. Captain Spry had sailed without me.

*\*\*\**

For a while I was dumbstruck. Finally I began to look about, and accosted a nearby wharfman. When I asked if he knew anything of the whereabouts of the trow *Lady Ann*, he nodded.

'She struck out last night, sir, on the tide. Never lingers very long, that one.' He glanced at my pack, then: 'Were you seeking a passage upriver?'

I nodded absently, my mind in a whirl. Soon I found my gaze straying to the spot where the trow's cargo had been placed... and saw it was still there, covered with sheets. In fact, the stacks had grown to more than twice the previous number, presumably the entire contents of the hold. I turned back to the wharfman, who was about to move off.

'Do you know the Dutch ship, by any chance? I speak of the merchantman, the *Waarheid.*'

The fellow gave another nod. 'Who don't know her. She's been a-lading here for days... sailing soon, I heard.'

'Do you know where she's bound?' I asked at once. 'It isn't Constantinople, is it?'

But to my surprise, the answer was a shout of laughter.

'By the Christ, sir, you're off by a mile. Constantinople?' He chuckled again. 'I can't recall the last time a vessel sailed for there - not from Bristol, anyways.' But seeing my confusion, the fellow shook his head.

'The *Waarheid*'s for Hamburg... not quite so far, eh?'

He left me, still shaking his head. And Justice Belstrang could only turn and retrace his steps, away from the harbour towards the nearest tavern.

The sun was just rising, and the place had not yet opened. But seeing me peering somewhat forlornly through the window, the host appeared, unbolted the door and gestured for me to enter. Gratefully I went in and took a seat, saying I would take a morning draught when he was ready. The man went about his business, leaving me to ponder my circumstances.

Well, the matter was plain enough: Spry had abandoned me, letter of passage or no. How much my poking about the day before had prompted such action, I did not know. But one fact at least had emerged: that the cannons taken to the Dutch merchantman, behind the backs of the soldiers, were not destined for the Grand Turk after all – but for Hamburg. In heaven's name, what did that mean?

I was in ignorance, I realized – almost as much as when I had first ridden into Lydney. But for the present my needs were plain: I must return there soon. Leucippus was in the stable at The Comfort - and I no longer believed I could trust Hawes, or anyone else in that place. Peck's death had shaken me, as much as the painful warning I had received the same night.

All of this I mulled over, fortified eventually by bread and cheese and a mug of beer. The sun was up, and customers began drifting into the tavern. Finally I summoned my faculties, paid the host and made my way outside again. My first thought was to return to the inn where I had stayed and see if the chamber was free for another night, or even two; as yet I was unsure how I was to make my way back up the Severn. But first, compelled by the noise of the busy port, I found myself wandering down to the quay again, ending up beside the covered cannon left by the *Lady Ann* – where I stopped abruptly: the porters were back. Or at least one of them was, the same fellow, I believed, whom I had last seen sitting nonchalantly upon one on the stacks. As I drew near, the man was quickly alert. It was time for some more invention.

'Minding Captain Spry's goods, are you?' I asked, adopting William Pride's blunt tone. And when he merely blinked, I added: 'I sailed in with him… I'm a friend of the Mountfords.'

But the name appeared to mean nothing. Rough-clad, muscular and sunburned, the man frowned and asked what I wanted from him. On impulse, I decided to say nothing of what I had seen the previous day. Instead I asked if he knew where I might find a vessel going up the Severn, whereupon the reply came readily enough.

'You could ask Darrett. His trow will sail in today.'

'Indeed?' I managed a smile of thanks. 'That's good to know... will he moor up here?'

I gestured towards the empty berth where the *Lady Ann* had been, to which the man merely gave a shrug. After that he waited, with a look that said I should leave him to his work. But I lingered.

'I saw the unloading,' I said in a casual tone, nodding towards the stacked ordnance. 'Heavy toil, eh?'

The other said nothing, but his impatience was growing.

'How long will it lie here?' I persisted. 'I don't see anyone guarding it, save you.'

A moment passed, while the porter looked me up and down with unconcealed distrust. But just as he was on the point of uttering some rebuff, or so I believed, there came a shout from some distance away. He looked round - as did I, to see two men approaching, making their way along the crowded quay. One of them was a porter, another of those I had observed shifting cannons the day before.

The other was Yakup.

My instinct was to turn about at once and make myself scarce – but it was too late. The Turk had seen me, and recognition was immediate. Briefly he slowed his pace, then walked forward swiftly – and very soon I was the object of all three men's attention. Thinking fast, I nodded a greeting.

'Master Yakup... I thought you had sailed on the trow.'

But my answer was a cold silence. There we stood, as ill-assorted a company as could be imagined. The porters glanced at each other, then back at me... whereupon the man I had first spoken with put on a blank stare, and moved his hand deliberately to his belt. I glanced down swiftly, expecting to see a poniard, but there was only a stubby oak billet - plain and serviceable, yet in skilled hands, just as deadly.

There was no remedy. Wordlessly I stepped back, turned and

left them. After I had walked a few yards I looked over my shoulder to see the porters had turned their backs and were in close conference. But Yakup stood apart, looking hard at me... and at once Russell's words came to mind, back at the Crickepit foundry: *I'd keep a wary eye on that one.*

Ill-at-ease, I left the quays and made my way back to the inn – only to learn that my chamber had already been bespoken, and there was no other room free.

Whereupon, when I consoled myself at a corner table with a cup of strong sack, the matter I had managed to forget returned abruptly – with such force that I almost bowed down with its weight.

I could still lose Thirldon. And here I was many miles away, friendless, on foot and likely in danger too. It was as low a moment as I had known, in many days.

***

And yet, even when a man is at his lowest ebb, solace may come in ways unexpected; even as I write it, I can feel the relief I felt that day. For late that afternoon, making my way cautiously back to the harbour – and I confess, somewhat the worse for the drink I had taken – I was surprised to find that the words spoken by the taciturn porter were true. Moored at the same berth previously occupied by the *Lady Ann* was another Severn trow, smaller and higher in the water, her sails tight-furled. As I drew near, I read the name painted about the prow – and almost laughed: she was called the *Last Hope*.

I stood a while, looking for signs of activity, before throwing caution to the winds and walking up the gangplank with my pack. When I glanced at the hold, I saw that it was but half-filled, its contents covered – and there was little doubt in my mind, from its shape, that the cargo was similar to Spry's: cannon, tightly packed.

This time, however, it was of no interest. I turned to the aft awning, screened by sailcloth, and called aloud for Captain Darrett, prompting voices from within. A head appeared - and I moved forward, to beg a passage back to Lydney.

To bring that matter to a close, after some conversation it was granted, and at a comfortable price. Whereupon I smiled in relief, to which the lugubrious-looking trow-master merely grunted. He was a sour fellow, I decided.

But in that too-brief judgement of the man's character, I would find, I had made another error.

## EIGHT

The *Last Hope,* I soon discovered, was an Upstream Trow: to whit, one which usually sailed up the Severn as far as Worcester, unlike the *Lady Ann* which was a Downstreamer. She was of shorter beam, and lighter in build. Captain Darrett rarely came to Bristol, it seemed. I had told him of my connection with the Mountfords, which drew a glum response.

'I'm carrying the scrag-end of their whoreson shipment,' he muttered. 'I'll be glad to see the back of it… the *Last Hope*'s not fitted out for such.'

He gestured vaguely to the cargo, as we stood on deck. Evening was drawing in, but the port was still abuzz. The sheeting was gone, and preparations were already in train for Darrett's cargo to be unloaded, to join the other cannons stacked on the quayside. His freight was smaller guns, minions and falcons. Finding him a man who was at least willing to talk, William Pride set to.

'Where's the shipment bound for, then?' I asked casually. 'London, or…?

'I couldn't say, for I don't ask,' came the reply. 'I'm content taking timber upriver to Gloucester or Tewkesbury, as a rule. I'm a peaceful man - carrying cannons makes me nervous.'

I nodded in understanding fashion, then asked when he expected to make sail back up the Severn. The next afternoon, I was told, whatever the tide. Captain Darrett, it seemed, was a countryman born and bred, who disliked cities. In truth, he seemed to dislike most things. Choosing my moment, I ventured to ask him about accommodation for the night, to which he eyed me above drooping moustaches, his beard thin and greying.

'You mean you want to sleep here, onboard?' And when I indicated assent, he sighed wearily.

'Well, if you must. You'll have my two crewmen for

company... I've a berth on shore. Once we're on the river, there will be four – nay, five of us. We'll be squashed up like stockfish... you'll have to shift for yourself. And I'll ask you to lay aside your sword.'

I offered my thanks, then frowned. 'Five of us? Besides you and I and your men, who is the other?'

To which, the answer came as something of a shock. 'There's a fellow going back to Purton with us. A foreigner name of Yakup, or so I'm told.'

With that the captain left me. I made my way to the stern, ducked beneath the awning and found a place to stow my pack. I then sat down heavily against the gunwale, with grim forebodings about the voyage ahead.

Captain Darrett's habitual gloom, I found, was catching.

***

The voyage out of Bristol, down the Avon and out into the Severn was uneventful enough. I had spent a tolerable night under the awning with Darrett's crewmen, who left me in peace. The following day I had been ashore to eat and drink, paying discreet attention to the unloading of the *Last Hope*, which proceeded apace. I did not stay to look for the porters; I knew enough about where at least a part of the ordnance from both trows was going. Nor did I question Darrett further, for I discovered he knew little of the Mountfords' business and cared even less. Once on the water, I was far more concerned with keeping an eye on my unwelcome fellow-passenger.

From the very start, Yakup ignored me. While I kept to the stern, or moved about the deck betimes, he remained seated in the prow of the vessel: a silent figure, gazing ahead. I was nonplussed as to why the Turk was travelling with us, having assumed he was leaving England with the cannons. And yet, the Dutch merchantman was bound for Hamburg, not Constantinople... here was a mystery that still confounded me.

Yakup and Darrett did not appear to know each other, and rarely spoke; nor did the crew appear to like the man. How we were all supposed to spend the night together, crammed beneath the awning, I could not imagine; hence I had already resolved to sleep on deck once again, as I had done aboard the *Lady Ann*. At least I could admire the Great Comet, still burning its way across the night sky. How long was it since I had first seen it, in the garden at Thirldon... a fortnight?

But by the afternoon I was restless. Being unladen, the trow moved swiftly enough upstream on a south-west breeze, and the following day we would be docking at Purton, yet my discomfort only increased. There was silence aboard the *Last Hope*, unlike that on the *Lady Ann* with the ill-tempered Spry bawling at his men. Captain Darrett was generally on deck, pointing his hangdog features ahead as we forged upriver.

Slowly the Severn narrowed, both banks now visible as the sun began to fall. I ate supper with the crewmen, sharing a pie I had bought in Bristol; and there was a small keg of beer in the stern, which was most welcome. Having stated my intention of sleeping on deck, I comforted myself with the thought that this night would be the last I ever spent on a boat - of any sort, anywhere. Hence, by the time dusk came and we dropped anchor close to the shoreline, I was in better spirits, my only concern being that it would not rain.

It did not, but it would have made little difference if it had. For the events of that night and what came after will remain with me, I believe, for the rest of my days.

The water was calm enough; just a light swell, which I had almost grown used to. All was quiet under the canopy at the stern, just an occasional snore which was almost reassuring. For a while I lay on my back under a blanket loaned by the crew, contemplating the heavens and, as always, finding my thoughts drifting homeward. But I was forced to stay those: worries about

Thirldon threatened to overwhelm me, and could leave me unable to sleep. Instead I thought on my quest, now somewhat mudded, to uncover what had happened to Richard Mountford's lamented brother. Thus far, I realised, I had found no evidence of treachery: only rumours and evasion, and a tangled tale of clandestine shipments of gunnery. I thought briefly of Tobias Russell and the Willets - and poor Thomas Peck. How much longer I should spend in Lydney, I did not know; I was eager to return home to find out whether my son-in-law George had made any progress in London.

I believe those were my last thoughts before I drifted off to sleep... only to wake with a jerk, my senses jangling.

To this day, I know not how I avoided the blow. Some instinct from the time of my restless youth, perhaps - or more likely I had heard a creak of boards. All I can say is that as I awoke I snapped my head aside, dimly aware of a shape looming over me - and heard a loud thud as something struck the timbers an inch from my neck. The next moment my hand flew out to grasp the arm that went up, ready to strike again – and then I was embroiled in a struggle for my very life. For a man of any age, it would have been hard enough - for one of my years, it was desperate.

Gasping aloud, I was forced to use all my strength just to keep my assailant from getting a hand about my throat - let alone using the billet he wielded. But this soon dropped to the deck, to be replaced by something deadlier. In the dim moonlight, I caught the flash of a blade – and on a sudden I was shouting for aid while I gripped the man's wrist, struggling to avoid being impaled. The dagger was long, its point only inches from my neck – and by now, I was in no doubt who was trying to kill me.

'Darrett!' I yelled. 'For pity's sake, will someone come?'

An oath that I did not understand flew from the lips of my attacker. While still trying to force his blade downwards, with his other fist he slammed me in the ribs. Winded, both hands shaking as I held his wrist, I let out a grunt of pain... and realised that I was losing the fight. Yakup was strong, and determined. So - was this how I would meet my death, I wondered? At the hands of a silent stranger?

With what strength remained I fought him, bringing up a knee to dig into his ribs, but to no avail. He was astride me now, pinning me to the gunwale, my head on the hard boards. The poniard hovered, trembling as we both strove for mastery of it... whereupon to my immense relief came shouts and hurried footfalls - and in a moment, it was over.

Strong arms seized my tormentor, dragging him away in the gloom. I heard muffled curses, a blow or two, and the blessed sound of the knife falling to the deck. Then I was forcing myself up on my elbows, shaking and panting... until a lantern appeared, and another figure loomed over me.

'Are you hurt?'

Captain Darrett was peering down, his jowly features drawn into a frown. 'What in God's name were you-'

'He tried to kill me!' I exclaimed breathlessly, gesturing at my assailant. And there was Yakup on his knees, held at the shoulders by the *Last Hope*'s burly crewmen, arms about his stomach where a blow had been delivered. He too was breathing hard, but his eyes were cast down.

'By the Christ.'

I looked up sharply to see the Captain nodding. Before I could speak, he added: 'I had a feeling he was up to something... I was asked to take him, though I didn't know why.' He threw a look at the man in question, who refused to meet his eye, then turned back to me.

'You must have upset someone mightily, Master Pride. I won't ask who that is... but no-one attempts murder on my vessel.' He straightened himself, drew a breath and addressed his men.

'Get some rope and bind this varlet up, good and tight,' he ordered. 'What happens after can wait until morning.' Facing me again, he put out a hand. I took it, and was hauled to my feet with a strength that surprised me.

'You and that one had best change places,' he muttered. 'My fellows will keep a watch on him, while you're coming under cover with me. I'll wager you need a drink… am I right?'

To which I could only nod, letting out a long breath. I was about to give my unlikely saviour a smile of gratitude; but seeing his familiar doleful expression returning, I forbore to do so, and followed him.

\*\*\*

The following days would bring revelations that astounded me – but once again I leap ahead in my tale. First let me speak of Captain Darrett, a man I had so carelessly misjudged.

He was a countryman as I have said, of a humble family, beholden to the Forest of Dean landowners as were so many. But he was not, I learned to my satisfaction, in the pay of Tobias Russell; nor did he owe allegiance to the Mountfords. He plied his river trade as his father had done, taking whatever cargo came to hand. He knew the foundries, of course, but rarely took their cannons, and only when the price was high enough. He had harboured misgivings about this return voyage, he admitted - not least when he had encountered the *Lady Ann* on the river on his way down to Bristol, and lowered sails to receive news from Captain Spry. He knew the man well enough, he said, though the two had never been friends.

'But I came alongside, and heard him out. He gave me a fee, asked me to meet our friend the Turk at Bristol Quays and bring him back upriver. It was a favour, he said, that would not be forgotten.' He sighed gloomily. 'Now I see that I should have said no… but money's money.'

I made no reply. We stood before the awning in the early morning, the *Last Hope* still rocking at anchor. I knew Darrett would not delay his return to Purton for long – but there was the small matter of the man who was now his prisoner, seated on the deck trussed like a fowl. I glanced towards him now and then, and received cold looks in return. The moment he was free, I feared, Yakup would again try to snuff out my life.

'Then, you know nothing of him?' I asked Darrett, watching him closely. I was falling into Belstrang habits, alert for any sign of duplicity.

The other shook his head. 'Only that he's a foreigner. I don't even know what tongue he speaks, for he never opens his mouth.' He paused, then: 'Why in God's name did he try to kill you? Do you truly not know?'

I hesitated; it was another turning point, I see now, yet at the time I was uncertain what to do. But for better or worse, I had decided to trust this dour trow-master... or perhaps I was merely tired of playing William Pride. Hence, I drew a breath and met his eye.

'I might have a notion. And I owe you an explanation – as surely as I know you and your crew saved my life last night. So, shall I make my explanations now, or do you prefer to make sail and head for Purton? The choice is yours.'

Some time passed while he considered; he was not a hasty man. His crew were on deck ready to raise anchor, eying him with puzzlement at the delay. Finally he nodded to them, threw a look at the bound figure of Yakup, and turned to me again.

'We'll sail now,' he said. 'But there's no reason you can't tell your tale as we go, is there? I hope it's worth the hearing – and more, I hope it'll set my mind at rest a little. For I've never had a would-be murderer for a passenger before... nor do I intend to carry one again.' He paused, then: 'So, Master Pride, will you get yourself out of the way, and leave us to our business?'

'I will, Master Darrett, and gladly,' I answered. 'But henceforth you may call me by my true name. I'm not William Pride – and I'm relieved to bid the man farewell as we speak. I'm Robert Belstrang, of Thirldon by Worcester: former Justice, and in pursuit of the same. And I'm in your debt.'

Whereupon I moved to the stern, out of his way. As I went, I saw him gazing after me in astonishment.

An hour or so later, after a riverman's breakfast and a mouthful of ale, the two of us sat close together under the awning. And while the Severn's banks drifted by in September sunshine, I gave the man a brief account of my business from first arrival at Lydney. Already it seemed an age ago, and yet my purpose was unfulfilled. It took less time than I feared, and I was heard in silence. Finally, the trow-master fixed me with one of his gloomy looks.

'So... when all's said and done, sir, you're a man of the law,' he murmured. 'In which case, I'll be mighty glad to hand the prisoner over to your charge. And the sooner the pair of you are off my vessel, the easier I shall be.'

'I understand,' I said. 'You have my thanks, now and always. Moreover, I shall try to arrange some reward for what you've done.' But as the other took in the words, I looked away; a different sort of burden was upon me. Once ashore and alone, I wondered, how was I to deal with my would-be assassin – let alone question him?

Yet question him I must: for here, I suspected, I would at last find some answers to the conundrum that gnawed at me. It was a sobering thought – then as I turned it about, a solution arose that lifted my spirits.

'Captain,' I said, turning to him. 'Supposing I had a proposition for you? A business one, I mean.' And ignoring the frown that appeared, I ploughed on. 'What if I prevailed upon you to take me a deal further upriver – past Purton, all the way to Gloucester. You make the voyage often, do you not? There you can discharge your present cargo - the prisoner, that is – into my keeping. In the meantime, I will swear out a warrant for his arrest. I'm acquainted with the Justice there - Thomas March, a good man. Hence you'll have performed a public service, and will be paid for it. What do you say?'

And I waited in trepidation while the other merely stared… before relief arrived, along with his sigh of acceptance.

'By the Lord,' Darrett groaned. 'I knew there was some doom hovering about, before I even left Purton. Now I'm conveying a man to the gallows… and there's rain on the way too. By the time we get to Gloucester we'll be swamped.'

But I was smiling, for I could not help it. And my smile merely widened when the man got stiffly to his feet, thrust aside the sheeting and gestured vaguely to the heavens.

'That whoreson comet's brought naught but trouble to the world,' he muttered. 'I'll be glad to see the back of that, too.'

## NINE

Two days later, on a wet Monday afternoon, the *Last Hope* sailed into Gloucester.

The rain, as Darrett predicted, had begun the previous day – a very gloomy Sabbath. By the time we drifted up the narrowing river and past the tiny island that divides it, everyone on board was wet to the bone. Though it barely troubled captain and crew, who were accustomed to all weathers. Finally we struck sail and eased alongside the city quay, where men stood to catch the thrown ropes. A short while later I was stepping on to solid ground, relieved that this part of my adventure, at least, was ended. When I finally returned to Lydney, I resolved it would be on horseback.

But for now, there was work ahead – chiefly with regard to my prisoner, his hands bound tightly behind him, who was being escorted off the boat by Darrett's crewmen. Having asked them to stay a moment, I quickly found a boy and paid him to fetch a constable. After he had scurried off, I turned to take farewell of the captain. As we shook hands, watched by curious onlookers, he jerked his head towards the sullen-faced Yakup.

'I'm curious to know what you find out about him – if he ever speaks,' he said. 'I marvel at his boldness, to do what he did. Likely he meant to knock you out cold with the billet and heave you overboard. Come morning, who could say what had happened, you being a clumsy landsman and all? And no spring chicken either - I'll wager he never expected you'd put up a fight.'

I gave him a wry smile. 'True enough. I thank you most heartily - and I will seek you out when I return to Lydney. But for now, here's the reckoning for my passage, with a little for the crew on top.'

I opened my purse and proffered the shillings, which Darrett took with a nod. As he turned to go back to his vessel, he paused. 'See now, will you not need witnesses to what occurred? Or is the word of an ex-Justice enough?'

'I believe it will be, in this case,' I answered, after a moment's thought. 'Once he's confessed who ordered him to put an end to my life – likely for poking about where I wasn't wanted. In that matter, I'm as curious as you are.'

Now, there was no more to be said. I watched the gloomy trow-master step away to speak briefly to his men. Then he was walking the gangplank on to his vessel, to disappear from sight. And a short while later, when the constable came puffing on to the quayside, I took farewell of the crew of the *Last Hope*, who delivered the prisoner into his hands and followed their captain back on board.

By now a small crowd had gathered, staring at the oddly-dressed captive who was seated on the wet ground with eyes lowered. Mercifully, the rain was easing off. The constable, meanwhile, having checked the prisoner's bonds, drew close and addressed me.

'Will you tell me what's occurred, sir?' He was a heavy-built man of middle years, perspiring heavily. 'And do you have a warrant against this man?'

Indeed I did, I told him, producing the scrap of paper I had managed to scrawl out aboard the *Last Hope*, with an old quill loaned by Darrett. As I handed it over I made my explanation in brief, prompting a frown from the officer.

'The charge is attempted murder?' He looked up from the paper and eyed the prisoner. 'Who is he?'

I told him what little I knew.

'Then I must convey him to the castle, into the hands of Master Gwynne. Will you come too, and tell him what you've told me?'

'I will,' I said with a sigh. 'Then I'll get out of these sodden clothes. I intend to seek out Thomas March – I assume he is still Justice here?'

'He is, sir,' the other answered. 'Do you know him?'

I nodded, impatient to be moving. Sensing my humour, the constable drew a truncheon from his belt and stepped towards Yakup, who tensed visibly. His gaze flew about, and for a moment I feared he would try and make some attempt at escape. But it was impossible: from all sides people regarded him with suspicion, if not hostility. The next moment he was hauled to his feet, stumbling as he stood up. And the silver charm at his belt swayed with him: the hand of Fatima, which was supposed to bring good luck to the wearer.

But Yakup's luck, seemingly, had run out.

\*\*\*

The old castle at Gloucester, long fallen into disrepair, is now used solely as a prison. It is close to the riverside, which meant that our walk was short. The prisoner was marched up to the gate, where a turnkey admitted us. Then we were entering the stone keep and tramping a dark passage until our charge was placed in a cell along with other men: there was no other choice, I learned. With no small relief to be rid of him, I then followed the constable to the keeper's chamber, where a low fire burned despite the mild weather.

Here I made myself known to Master Daniel Gwynne. I was facing a cold, sallow-faced man, who somehow put me in mind of a lizard. Yet he was a gentleman of sorts, in passable clothes and a small if ill-fitting ruff about his long neck, who greeted me formally before gesturing me to a stool. As I sat down, I realised how long it was since I had set my rump on anything padded... that at least, was some comfort.

'Belstrang?' The keeper peered at me across his table. 'I seem to recall the name, sir... will you enlighten me?'

I gave my former station at Worcester, and mentioned my

acquaintance with Justice March, which produced a curt nod. Still in my damp clothes, I then provided the man with a concise account of events since my leaving Lydney, precisely a week before. Having ended the tale with Yakup's attempt on my life, I awaited his response.

'A Turk, you say?' Gwynne was frowning. 'Sent by the Sultan, to oversee a secret shipment of cannons. I confess I find that hard to believe.'

'So did I,' I answered. 'And there's a deal more to say about it, too.' I was thinking of the Dutch merchantman in Bristol and what the wharfman had told me, about the vessel being bound for Hamburg. In my weariness I allowed these thoughts to distract me, before realising that the keeper was now regarding me suspiciously.

'Yet such trade is not against the law, is it?' He enquired. 'With Constantinople, I mean. As far as I'm aware, we are not at war with the Grand Turk.'

I reminded him that the Mountford Foundries were in the service of the King, and as far as I knew, all their ordnance was supposed to be sent to the Royal Armouries at the Tower. I was on the point of telling him about the *Waarheid*'s destination too, but for some reason I did not.

'Well, it's a weighty business,' the keeper allowed. 'But you may count on me. I'll question your Turk, and then decide on my best course.'

'I would like to attend the interrogation,' I said. 'I want to know why – or rather, on whose orders – the man tried to kill me.'

But the other was displeased by that. 'It's my place, sir,' he murmured, his reptilian eyes fixed on mine. 'I have my means, which are private.'

At that, I stiffened. 'Do you mean you'll put him to hard question? I would remind you that torture is illegal in this country, without license from the King.'

'Thank you, Master Belstrang,' came the sardonic reply. 'I believe I too know the law.'

With that, he sat back and waited; the meeting was over, and I was expected to withdraw. And yet, with true Belstrang stubbornness, I remained seated.

'I insist on being present when the prisoner is questioned,' I said. 'I need to get to the nub of this matter, for the sake of Sir Richard Mountford as well as for my own peace of mind. If necessary, I will seek leave from another authority.'

'Do you mean Justice March?' The other enquired coolly.

I signalled assent, then added that besides, I had been told Yakup spoke hardly any English. As a traveller, likely he used some other tongue, like Italian. I had some knowledge of it...

'Very well, if you insist upon it so forcefully.' Gwynne gave an impatient snort. 'I'll let him stew in the cell for the night, then begin the interrogation tomorrow at ten of the clock. Are you content now?'

To which I nodded, and rose to take my leave. As I reached the door, I glanced back to see the man busying himself with some papers. He did not look up.

Whereupon this bedraggled ex-magistrate got himself outside, asked directions to the house of the Justice, and trudged through the bustling city in search of some better company. And within the half hour, to my immense satisfaction I was made welcome – and more, there was no need to find an inn. For a while at least I was to be the guest of Thomas March, in whom I found an ally and a fellow-sceptic.

*\*\**

March was shrewd, and generally known for his rough humour, but he could also be a man of hot temper: a former officer, who had seen hard service in the Low Countries. I had not seen him in years, yet he was unchanged: a hotspur, who was inclined to mete out harsh sentences to miscreants. When I told him my tale that evening over a good supper, he was both intrigued and indignant. With him, I had spared no details - and by the time I was done, he was looking outraged.

'But this is treasonous,' he exclaimed. 'Mountford's people are supplying ordnance to a foreign power without the King's knowledge, let alone his license. Men are hung for less!'

I made no reply, for it was true. We were sitting at March's large table, about which his brood of children had once crowded. Now they were grown and gone, while his wife was away for the summer. Over a cup of Hippocras, we pondered the matter at length before my host spoke again.

'Hamburg... you're certain the Dutchman was bound for there?' He asked. And when I told him I had no reason to doubt the man who informed me, a frown appeared.

'But it makes no sense. From what that foundry-master told you – Russell, was it? – the ordnance goes to the Grand Turk. He swore you to secrecy, in your guise as Pride the speculator, on pain of death – so what are we to think? Since the King's peace, we're not at war with any nation on the continent - especially the German States.'

'I know,' I replied. 'And there's more to be uncovered – to whit the Concord Men, of whom Russell claimed ignorance. To my mind it sounds like a syndicate, diverting Mountford cannons from their rightful destination for private profit. I'd wager there are powerful men involved, who first put up the money - which means I could be on dangerous ground.'

March sighed, took a drink and met my eye. 'Men like you and I have rarely been short of enemies, have we?'

'We have not,' I agreed. 'Even if I haven't always been correct in distinguishing friend from foe.' After a brief silence, I added: 'Though there's no difficulty when it comes to the prisoner Yakup. Indeed, I'm lucky to be alive.'

At that, the other frowned. 'You and I should question him together,' he said. And before I could speak, he lifted a hand. 'I don't trust Gwynne, nor do I like his methods.' He put on a grim smile. 'They say I'm a hard man, but I've always tried to be a fair one. The keeper of the gaol is a bitter fellow, who feels he's worthy of higher things. And he's not above taking a bribe, I've heard. If your Turk serves these powerful men you speak of, then…'

He broke off, his meaning plain. In truth, it had never occurred to me that Yakup was in a position to pose any sort of difficulty – but his orders clearly came from somewhere. Having turned the matter about, I gave a nod.

'Well then, we must present ourselves at the castle by ten of the clock tomorrow, and face Master Gwynne together. Though I expect he'll insist on being part of the interrogation.'

'He can insist all he likes,' March replied sharply. 'But he knows I have the ear of the High Sheriff of Gloucestershire – Thomas Chester is a hawking man, like me.' A grin appeared. 'Whereas, if I recall correctly, fishing was always your sport. So – tomorrow we'll do a little fishing, shall we?'

With that he raised his cup, and we drank together.

\*\*\*

The morning dawned cloudy and windy, but Robert Belstrang had slept like a lamb: my first good night's rest since leaving The Comfort at Lydney. In dry clothes, with a fresh shirt loaned by my host, I felt ready to face whatever the day brought – and more, for the first time I believed I might make some headway in this tangled affair. Having breakfasted, Justice March and I left the house and walked to the castle, prepared for a confrontation with the keeper. But on arrival, here was the first surprise of the day: the interrogation, it seemed, was already in progress – and had been for the best part of an hour.

'What in God's name do you mean, fellow?'

March was staring belligerently at the hapless guard who stood in our way. We were outside the keeper's chamber - the door of which was wide open, showing that the room was empty.

'Your pardon, Master Justice,' the man answered, with growing unease. 'Master Gwynne is not to be disturbed when questioning a felon...' but seeing March's anger, he broke off.

'I'll decide who's a felon and who isn't!' The Justice roared. 'The interrogation was to be at ten of the clock – so my friend Justice Belstrang was told, and he is expected.'

With a gulp, the guard glanced at me. 'I know naught of that... I have my orders, and-'

'And I'm giving you new orders,' March broke in. 'You will convey us to where the prisoner is being questioned without further delay, or answer for the consequences. Do you understand?'

The man managed a nod. 'Very well, sir... but we must leave the castle and walk some distance.' Seeing we did not understand, he added: 'Master Gwynne sometimes questions prisoners at his house nowadays, for privacy's sake. It's by St Michael's - If you'd care to follow me...'

But once again he was obliged to break off, as March gave an impatient sigh. 'I know where he lives,' he grunted. Turning to me, he said: 'Let's make haste, shall we?'

And so we did, walking briskly through windswept streets, swords rattling and cloaks blowing in the best traditions of gentlemen in a hurry. Within a short time we had made our way to the other side of Gloucester, with the East Gate ahead. Here we stopped outside an imposing enough house, on the door of which March knocked loudly. Turning to me, he said:

'Do you recall that devil Topcliffe, Queen Elizabeth's interrogator?' And when I nodded: 'Kept a room in his own house, I heard, fitted out with irons and Christ-knows-what implements of torture. They say he enjoyed it – I've half a mind to think Daniel Gwynne is following his example.'

I was about to make some rejoinder when the door was opened by a servant. Henceforth, after a few curt words from March, the two of were conveyed to a chamber at the rear. The lackey was on the point of knocking at the closed door, but to his alarm March pushed past him and threw it open. We entered - and stopped in our tracks.

The room was bare, without windows or adornment, lit by candles and an iron brazier in which coals burned. Against one wall was a rough bench with a number of tools upon it: pincers, hammers and the like. While in the centre was a heavy chair to which the familiar figure of Yakup, now dishevelled and looking far less dangerous than when I had last seen him, was bound tightly, his legs shackled. As March and I entered, there came a muttered oath, and a man in shirt sleeves whirled about.

But it was not Gwynne. Instead we saw a hard-faced man with the look of an ex-soldier, his long hair tied back. He would have spoken, but at sight of our garb he hesitated - whereupon another voice sounded from close by.

'Master Justice... and Master ex-Justice. What an honour.'

I looked round sharply to see Gwynne himself, seated on a stool and regarding the two of us with his lizard's gaze. As we faced him, he rose and gestured vaguely towards the man who was now his helpless victim.

'You're somewhat late... did I not say that I would begin work at nine of the clock?'

'You know perfectly well you did not,' I returned, my own indignation growing. 'Nor did you inform me that you meant to remove the prisoner from the castle and bring him here. I demand an explanation-'

'Save your breath, sir.'

It was March, standing beside me, who cut me short. Casting a gaze from Gwynne to his interrogator and back, he held in his anger with an effort, then:

'I intend to question this man,' he said, pointing. 'I demand that you release him at once into my charge, and have him returned to the gaol. You may protest your rank, or employ any argument you choose, but I will answer to the High Sheriff for my actions. At the castle we'll do things properly, in the room generally used for such purposes – and I don't need any help from this one.'

He indicated the interrogator, who was watching us stonily. There followed a brief silence, but the matter was settled. Though Gwynne's resentment was plain, he knew he was on unsafe ground. Wordlessly he signalled to the ex-soldier to release his charge, then watched blank-faced as Yakup stood up, his eyes fixed on me. Perhaps, I reflected later, we had arrived not a moment too soon: the man looked unharmed, even if his clothes were grimy and soaked with sweat.

Yet there was no hint of gratitude or of relief in the dark eyes that met mine: only a defiant stare. It would be some time, I knew, before this man made a confession. How that was to be achieved, I was uncertain - but I did not intend to give up until he did.

## TEN

An hour later, in a bare, cramped room at the castle, the interrogation began.

There was no guard present: March had ordered it, as he had demanded that he and I alone should examine the prisoner, much to Gwynne's annoyance. But seeing how determined we were he relented, seemingly washing his hands of the affair. Hence, I at last faced the man who had almost succeeded in killing me, fixing him with a hard look which seemed to trouble him not at all. Standing before us as we sat behind a small table, his hands still bound, he assumed an air of passive calm.

'So, you speak no English, I'm told?' March enquired in a bland tone. And when the other did not react: 'How do you talk to your masters - in Italian?'

Again there was no response, whereupon my fellow startled me by uttering words I did not recognise. It sounded like '*Adin ne?*' And when Yakup merely blinked, he added: '*Efendin kim?*'

A moment passed, in which I believed I saw a flicker of uncertainty in our prisoner's gaze, but it soon vanished.

'That's odd,' March said, half-turning to me. 'This man doesn't seem to speak Turkish either. I asked him his name, and that of his master.'

'Are you certain?' I asked, non-plussed.

March's answer was to deliver another, longer question in Turkish, which I will not attempt to reproduce. The reaction was the same, and I began to believe he was right: Yakup did not appear to understand a word.

'Well, I'm confounded,' I said. 'Where did you acquire your knowledge of that language?'

'From mercenaries... a few phrases,' came my companion's reply. He gazed intently at the prisoner, who stared back.

'Shall I try some Italian?' I ventured. 'I hear it's the *lingua franca* on the Mediterranean.'

'You could,' March replied. 'But I have another idea.' Whereupon he cleared his throat noisily, and addressed Yakup in another language entirely.

'*Cuál es tu nombre? Podemos hablar español si quieres.*'

The reaction was instant: Yakup stiffened, but recovered at once – and yet it was enough. I turned to March, to see him wearing a little smile of satisfaction.

'Just a notion, Robert,' he murmured. 'Can you not tell the difference between a Turk and a Spaniard? Or do all foreigners look alike to you?'

'Good God...' I eyed Yakup. 'It never occurred to me. I was told by Captain Spry he was Turkish, so...'

But I broke off: Spry had told me the man's name, yet in truth he had never actually said he was Turkish. Was it merely the silver hand of Fatima that had convinced me, I wondered?

'It's as good a cover as any,' March said. 'We may be at peace with Spain now, but old enmities don't die. If I were him I wouldn't want it bruited about either – not in England.'

'In which case,' I said, 'I'd wager he does know some English. How else could he have got by?'

In silent agreement, the two of us turned to face our captive, who was looking somewhat taut.

'You're not Yakup, are you,' March said. 'What shall I call you - Jacobo? The meaning's roughly the same, isn't it?' And when the other still made no answer: 'Did you think I wouldn't find you out? Your beard looks right, but your skin's the wrong shade. I should know - I've been acquainted with a few Turks, but I've been at close quarters with more Spaniards than I care to remember.'

He paused to let our prisoner digest his words, but I was thinking fast: on a sudden, the case was altered entirely. I thought briefly on what Russell had told me, back at Cricklepit. One notion occurred at once: since the Dutch Truce, trade with Spain was legal – but surely the Mountford foundries would not supply cannons to King Philip?

Then it struck me, like a blow to the skull. I thought of the *Waarheid* - the Dutch merchantman at Bristol, and drew a sudden breath.

'The Papists,' I said, staring at March. 'The forces of the Holy Roman Emperor. Close allies of Spain, of course... can it be possible?'

'What... do you speak of the troubles in Bohemia?' he asked sharply.

'By the Christ, I do.' I stared at Yakup – or whatever his name was. 'You're not overseeing shipments to the Grand Sultan, are you?' I demanded. 'That's why the ordnance was put on the Dutchman, destined for Hamburg. From there it could be carried south, through Anhalt...'

I faced March again. 'You spoke of it being illegal, supplying guns to foreign powers without leave - but this is far worse. As I understand it, the Archduke Matthias is sending troops to Bohemia to support the revolt, hence-'

'Hence your friends the Mountfords could have struck a bargain with him,' my fellow-justice finished. He looked shocked – and when he threw an angry look at our prisoner, the man looked away. Perhaps it was dawning on him what might befall him, if he was truly serving powers that were in conflict with the Elector Palatine: our own King's son-in-law.

'I think you'd better start talking to us – *señor*,' March said then, laying his hands on the table.

We waited, and for some considerable time. My expectation was that the Spaniard, as I now knew he was, would continue to remain silent for fear of incriminating himself. But somehow, we had to get him to speak: the stakes were now far higher –

indeed, it seemed there was a conspiracy to be uncovered, of immense proportions. I sensed March's growing impatience, and would have spoken up, when the prisoner surprised us.

'I am not Jacobo,' he said, in heavily accented English. 'If you wish, I will answer to Sebastien.'

The voice was deep, the words spoken haltingly. As both of us stirred, Sebastien's gaze flickered between us.

'I wish to make a bargain,' he added.

'Oh, you do?' In an instant, March's indignation rose. 'By the Christ, you've got some nerve, fellow... do you not understand the predicament you're in?'

'*Si*, I understand,' came the reply. 'But you want things from me, I want things in return. Free passage out of England, I must have.'

'Hah!' With an oath, March slapped a hand on the table. 'You're daydreaming, my friend. Is the sentence for spying not the same in Spain as it is here? Think!'

'Spying?' For the first time, the man showed unease. 'I am not an *espiar, señor*. I'm sent as observer, messenger...'

'No, Master Sebastien, that will not do.' March cut him short, raising a hand to point. 'A Spaniard going under an alias - that alone will condemn you, do you not see? And if I were to send you to London – to the Tower, no less – you would face very hard questioning indeed.' He paused, then: 'It may be that, if you still maintain your defence after such treatment, someone will believe you. But by then it will scarcely matter, for you'll be a broken man in every sense.'

It was a bluff, I knew: March had no desire to send the prisoner to London. I glanced aside, met his eye and understood that he wished me to chime in, perhaps playing the more lenient role. Since I still smarted from Sebastien's attempt on my life, however, I had other ideas.

'Who ordered you to kill me?' I snapped. And when the man

hesitated: 'I know Captain Spry passed a message to Captain Darrett when they met on the river, telling him to take you aboard. You knew what to do, didn't you?'

After a moment, the other lowered his gaze. 'It was a matter of business,' he admitted. 'I have no quarrel with you.'

'Business?' I echoed, my anger growing. 'I think Spry knew what had to be done, to stop me prying. He took it on himself to act, knowing his masters would approve – so I'll ask again. Who would give such an order?'

Whereupon, to my satisfaction the admission came at last, if unwillingly. Sebastien drew a breath, then: 'He is *capataz*... master of *la fundición* – the foundry. His name is Tobias.'

Russell, of course: now, I believed I had known it all along. Leaning forward, trying to rein in my eagerness, I then asked who Russell took orders from. But the answer was a shake of the head, and a firm denial.

'I only know the *capataz*. And Spry, and the sailors.'

'I don't believe you,' I retorted. 'And I demand here and now that you answer this: who are the Concord Men?' Whereupon I watched him closely, only to be disappointed.

'I don't know what you speak of.'

His face was blank, and he appeared to be telling the truth, yet I was unconvinced. With a sigh of impatience I leaned back, letting March take the reins again.

'Well, Master Sebastien, you are in difficulty still,' he said calmly. 'Whether under orders or not, attempted murder is a capital crime for which there is only one penalty, as a rule. You will hang - and without the chance to make your last confession, let alone receive the rites you would wish for. Do you compass that?'

There was another silence, which brought satisfaction to both March and myself: as Justices, we knew when we had begun to breach a man's resistance. For the first time Sebastien showed fear, whereupon I strove to drive home our advantage.

'Indeed... I suspect no priest in England would assist you, if he learned you pose as a Mahommedan,' I added. 'You even wear the hand of Fatima about your person. I wonder, do you have a blessing for what you do?'

But at that Sebastien gave a start - and on a sudden his face contorted in anger.

'I have blessing, I do!' He cried. 'You think to shame me? My masters do God's holy work in aiding our Emperor!' Breathing hard, he lifted his bound hands in a gesture of helpless rage. 'There is a war beginning, sirs – are you so stupid you do not know it? What happened in Prague has lit the flame... our armies are gathering, and will march in glory against the enemies of Christ. I would be proud to lose my life in that cause... and you may use threats as you please!'

With that he backed to the wall and sat down, lapsing into a sullen silence. It seemed we had misjudged him... or had we?

'Very well, I concur.'

To my surprise, March relaxed. Turning to me, he pretended to murmur a few words in my ear: mere gibberish, for the prisoner's benefit. Finally he whispered: 'One more shove and we'll have him,' before facing our quarry again.

'You have made your choice, Master Sebastien,' he said. 'I will not question you further. Instead I'll have you sent back to the cell. There you'll remain, with the other prisoners... I suspect by now you know what sort of men they are. However, I'll let it be known to them that you're a Spanish spy, awaiting sentence.' He put on a grim smile. 'There are ex-soldiers among them – and among the guards too, I seem to recall. Let's see what happens then, shall we?'

There followed a silence. Sebastien had tensed in every limb, his eyes on the floor. Yet we waited, allowing the notion to strike home. The man knew this was no idle threat, for it was achieved with ease - and what fate might befall him come night-time, at the hands of half a dozen ruffians who hated Spain, could be readily imagined.

At last he lifted his head, threw a baleful gaze from me to March and back, and spoke.

'You mistake, *señors*,' he said, speaking low. 'For you know not what trouble you bring, if you go against such people. I speak of *los Hombres de la Concordia.*' He paused, then: 'You are small men - but they are big, and would destroy you. And yet, I spoke of a bargain, so I offer this: there is one I know, because he came to *la fundición* often, and to the port. He is Francis Mountford... a cruel man. He slew his own uncle.'

Whereupon, with a slicing gesture, our prisoner signalled that he had told all he knew, adding: 'Now I ask one thing in return: that I remain Yakup the Turk in the prison. Will you not grant me this one mercy?'

We were both silent, exchanging looks. Sebastien was an enemy - yet he had his code and his faith, and no small degree of courage. Finally, March threw him a nod. Rising from the table, he threw the door open and called the guard. Whereupon, both on our feet, we watched as the servant of the Concord Men – that cabal of ruthless investors, who dared treat with England's enemies – was taken away.

'Well, sir,' March breathed, placing a hand on my shoulder. 'I suspect that, like me, you could do with a drink.'

\*\*\*

The inn was The Crown, where we took a good dinner, yet neither of us was content.

Once again, I had stumbled on a conspiracy – as I had done in London two years earlier, with the uncovering of the vile Anniversary Plot. In truth there are times, since I quitted the magistrate's bench, when I think trouble has sought Robert Belstrang out as some kind of punishment – even that life might be more peaceful were I still a Justice. But enough: a man must play the cards he has drawn. Sitting in a corner booth at the old inn, with a full stomach but a mind in turmoil, I reviewed the position with Gloucester's good Justice, thankful that he at least was a man of honesty – as was my old friend Sir Richard Mountford, I reflected sadly.

'How his son could have turned out to be such a varlet – a murderer, no less - is beyond me,' I said. 'Though I suspected John Mountford had found out what was being done at his family's foundries, and paid a cruel price for it, I never truly believed Francis could do that - or even order it.'

March shook his head, but said nothing.

'Now I've a task ahead that fills me with sadness,' I went on. 'To tell a friend what wickedness has been done behind his back... that he, one of the King's Founders of Ordnance, has unknowingly been supplying the armies of the Papists... it's direful.'

'And yet, it must be done.'

My friend took a drink, set it down and faced me. 'For now, I must inform the High Sheriff, who will inform the Privy Council in London. Meanwhile I'll swear out a warrant for the arrest of Russell and Captain Spry. Then I'll appoint men to ride down to Lydney and apprehend them.'

'And I will go with them,' I said at once. 'My horse is still in the stable at the inn... if you can loan me another, I would be in your debt.'

'Of course,' March nodded. 'You've done much to bring this foul business to light...' he paused, then: 'I should tell you that I won't inform Gwynne of what we've uncovered. As I've said, I don't trust him... nor do I know how long is the reach of these Concord Men.'

It was a sobering thought.

'I can scarcely believe it,' I said, turning it about. 'A nest of

traitors in the heart of England, intent on profit before country…
we must be sure of our ground, before making accusations. I
might have expected them to be Papists all, with some desperate
hopes of shifting power in Europe – but the Mountfords are not.
It can only be greed that drives Francis.'

'It was ever thus, was it not?' March said, with a wry look.
'But we are in agreement: I'll arrest the lackeys first – the small
fry like Russell. They can be questioned easily – but the big fish
will have to wait, likely until the Lord Chief Justice himself
orders their arrests.'

'And yet, aside from Francis Mountford,' I said, 'we don't
know who they are.'

We fell silent. Even a firebrand like March, I knew, could find
himself in water that was too deep for him. As for me, what was
I but an ex-Justice, with an inherent impatience towards
wrongdoers?

'Then again, we'll do no good sitting here,' I said, with an
effort. 'If I might beg another night's hospitality from you, I'll
set out as soon as your officers are ready – and I swear not to
return empty-handed.'

At that March managed a smile of approval, whereupon we
drained our mugs together. But as we rose to take our leave, I
confess to a pang of apprehension.

What might transpire when I returned to the Forest of Dean, I
had not the least idea.

## ELEVEN

The arresting party left Gloucester the following day, in bright sunshine. I rode a gelding borrowed from March, of whom I had taken my farewell early that morning. We had parted with few words, our purpose being clear enough. Meanwhile I had written a letter to Hester, attempting to explain my extended absence, which the Justice would see delivered. Thirldon seemed far away; and in the light of what had happened these past days, even my fears for its future had been eclipsed.

We were six in number, including myself and the party's leader, a sergeant-at-arms named Parry. The other men were constables chosen by Parry himself. A plain, far-sighted man, he knew the purpose of our journey, though not what lay behind it; as yet that was a matter only for March and myself. As we left the city and took the westward road for Highnam, with at least a twenty-mile journey ahead, he eased his mount alongside mine and spoke up.

'What sort of man is this Tobias Russell, sir? Will he prove troublesome?'

'He might,' I replied. 'He's no weakling, and he's used to giving orders. Indeed, so is the trow-master, Spry. But I'm certain that you and your men will prevail.'

'We must do so,' Parry said. 'Justice March is not a man to brook failure.'

I made no remark upon that. The night before, March and I had agreed that discretion must be our watchword. As far as Parry knew, Tobias Russell was to be arrested for conspiracy, in concealing the cause of death of John Mountford. Captain Spry was to be apprehended for ordering a grievous assault on my person by a man now in custody, believed to be a Turkish seaman. The constables, well-armed, were to render assistance as necessary. It was enough – and I could not help feeling a sense of satisfaction at the notion of seeing those two hard-faced men, Russell and Spry, being put in irons.

The journey passed without difficulty: from Highnam we rode south-westward through Westbury, Newnham and Blakeney, with the harvest still in progress in the fields. Then, as the day waned, we entered the Forest of Dean, falling into single file on the narrow road. At last, weary and saddle-sore, we reached Lydney and drew rein before The Comfort inn, the horses blowing and snorting in the afternoon haze. It was nine days since I had left here to sail downriver with Spry – but now, my first thought was for Leucippus. Dismounting quickly, I left the gelding in the care of Parry's men and hastened to the stable – only to receive a shock.

My beloved horse was gone.

In dismay I looked about, seeing only an old piebald nag in one stall; where Leucippus had been there was nothing but straw. Whereupon, gathering my wits, I went out and marched to the inn door. When I entered, the first person I encountered was Henry Hawes - who jumped as if he'd seen a ghost.

'Master Pride, sir...' he faltered. 'I... it's good to see you, after... or I should say, you're most welcome.'

We stared at each other. I was non-plussed by his manner – until a notion struck me with some force: the man had thought I was dead! Could Spry have told him of it, in the belief that Yakup had carried out his grisly task? More, had what occurred on the *Last Hope* not been reported? Darrett, I recalled, was no friend of Spry, or of the foundry men...

'You look somewhat pale, Master Hawes,' I said at last. 'Did you not think I would return? I left my horse, did I not?'

'Indeed... of course you did.' He swallowed, trying to gather himself. 'I've had the boy take him out for exercise a few times, seeing as more than a week's past, and...'

'I see,' I broke in, not believing a word of it. 'Perhaps you'd be good enough to tell me where he is now?'

'He's out in the forest, sir,' came the quick reply. 'If you'd like to make yourself at home, I'll send word. He'll soon be returned… and your chamber is free, as arranged. Have you had a long journey?'

On a sudden the host was all bustle, calling to his daughter to see that the gentleman's bed was aired. I must be hungry, he said – supper could be ready within the hour. Meanwhile, would I take a mug at the house's expense?

'Most cordial of you,' I said. 'But what of my friends outside? There's a sergeant and four constables, come all the way from Gloucester - thirsty men all. Shall I bring them in?'

Hawes gulped, before managing a nod. 'Indeed, sir… all are welcome at The Comfort.' But mention of officers of the law had caused him alarm – and on impulse, I decided to frighten the daylights out of him.

'I'll confess I wasn't honest with you when I was last here, Master Hawes,' I said, placing my hand on my sword-hilt for good measure. 'In truth, my name isn't Pride. It's Belstrang – former Justice Belstrang, magistrate of Worcester. I'm here on legal business, to assist with an arrest.'

To my satisfaction, it worked well enough. Hawes made no answer, but appeared to shrink somewhat. Finally he cleared his throat and asked: 'Might I enquire as to who is to be arrested, sir?'

'Well now…' I put on my bland look. 'You know how the land lies hereabouts, perhaps better than most. Why don't you hazard a guess?'

But we were interrupted, as the door swung open and Sergeant Parry walked in. Taking in his surroundings, he threw a glance from me to the hapless host and back.

'Is this someone you know, Master Belstrang?'

'It is,' I nodded. 'Henry Hawes is master of the Comfort, and a wellspring of intelligence too - or of gossip at least. Will you bring your men in, and we'll take supper together?' Turning to Hawes, I added: 'You offered such, did you not?'

'Well, mayhap I did...' he eyed Parry, forcing a weak smile. 'I pray you, seat yourself, master. There's a chine of beef, and some roasted woodcock-'

'That'll serve us well.' Without delay, Parry turned and went out again. Through the open door, voices could be heard along with the clink of harness. Feeling somewhat calmer, I looked about for a table, whereupon my eyes fell on the inn's only customer, sitting in a corner open-mouthed.

It was Jonas Willett, who had clearly heard every word.

'By the Lord...' he gazed at me, then gave a shake of his head. 'My boy had you down as a snooper of some kind, sir... but never a Justice. Or even an ex-Justice.'

'No matter, Master Willett.' I threw him a smile. 'My fellows and I have come to stir things up a little... perhaps when it's all over we'll take a mug together, shall we?'

And with that I sat myself down, stretched my tired limbs and looked forward to supper.

*\*\**

That evening, having seen his men billeted in the village, Parry conferred with me in a corner of the inn. It was quiet – too quiet. Word of our arrival had got round quickly, it seemed, and for the present most of the population of Lydney had stayed away. Even Jonas Willett, who had nothing to fear as far as I knew, had left soon after we had spoken.

'I intend to ride soon after daybreak,' the sergeant told me. 'If you'll be our guide, once we reach the foundry we'll dismount, then close in. How many men are there, do you know?'

'I'm unsure... a dozen, perhaps,' I answered. 'But they won't be armed as your men are. Once Russell's taken, I doubt the others will offer any resistance. To my knowledge they're owed wages, and are discontented.'

The other nodded, whereupon I rose and told him I had an errand: Leucippus had not yet been returned, and my unease was growing. Having looked about for Hawes without success, I went outside and walked to the stable, where a light showed. Hearing voices, I entered - and stopped.

Two men stood close together beside the stalls, squaring up to each other in angry fashion. One was Hawes, while the other looked familiar: a rough-clad, scowling fellow - whereupon recognition dawned. He was Combes, the man who had got the better of Thomas Peck, that night in the inn when I had stopped them fighting... the same night on which Peck had lost his life, and I had received that brutal warning. As I appeared both of them turned quickly, then fell silent.

'Master Hawes,' I said. 'I expected my horse to be here by now. It grows late, does it not?'

This time Hawes did not appear to have an explanation to hand; rather, he looked anxious. Taking a step away from the other man, he summoned an apologetic look. 'Your pardon, Master Pride – Master Belstrang, I should say. There has been a delay, and-'

'Delay?' It was Combes who spoke up, and harshly. 'Double dealing, I might call it.' He too took a pace forward, but on recognising me in turn, sword and all, he hesitated. Finally he asked: 'Did I hear you say *your* horse, sir?'

'You did,' I replied. 'Of what interest is it to you?'

The man paused again, then threw a belligerent look at Hawes, who refused to meet his gaze.

'You whoreson knave!' he spat. 'Why, the horse wasn't yours to sell!' His hand shot out, to grip the hapless host by his collar. The other hand came up too, balled into a fist...

'Enough!' I called out, hand on sword, in an echo of that other night when I had drawn it to such purpose. 'There's a sergeant-at-arms in the inn, and constables nearby. Go any further, and I'll have you arrested for affray.'

Another silence fell. Combes dropped his hand and let go of Hawes, who at once hurried towards me.

'I pray you, sir, let me explain,' he blurted. 'There's been a misunderstanding... nothing you need concern yourself about. The horse is safe and well-cared for, and-'

'So he is – and in my possession!'

Eyes blazing, Combes advanced towards us, pointing a finger. 'And it's I who'll do the explaining.' Mastering himself with difficulty, he faced me. 'This man offered me the horse, for ten sovereigns. I told him I had a buyer but would need to raise the money, so he said I could keep him for the present. He swore it was above board... settlement of an old debt.' He threw another baleful look at Hawes. 'Then, mayhap I was a fool for trusting one of Mountford's lackeys!'

I met his eye, but observed no guile: only righteous anger. Glancing at Hawes, I saw him fumbling for words... and now I understood. Striving to keep my own temper, I took a step back, drew my rapier and levelled it – not at Combes, but at the landlord.

'I had a notion you'd thought I was dead,' I said. 'That's what Spry told you, wasn't it - that I'd been dealt with on the river, and wasn't coming back? And was my mount your reward, for services rendered?' Drawing a breath, I fixed the man with my hardest look. 'I could have you charged with horse-stealing - do you know what the penalty is?'

Silence fell. Hawes was stock-still, eyes lowered - then he jumped: a rapid sideways movement, by which he meaned to duck past me to the door. But Combes was quicker: his meaty hand shot out again to grasp the host's arm, then he was flung to the stable floor to sprawl in the straw. Upon which I leaned forward, pointing my blade at his neck.

'Let's go into the inn, shall we?' I suggested. 'The sergeant might want to ask you a few questions – as do I.'

I turned to Combes. 'My thanks for your assistance,' I said, 'and my condolences for the way you've been deceived. If you'll bring my horse back here now, and see him well bestowed, I'll pay you something for your trouble.'

The other hesitated, then let out a long breath. 'Well then, it's I who'll thank you,' he allowed. 'For I would have purchased a stolen beast, and...' He trailed off, frowning at Hawes who was sitting up, a sickly look on his features. 'Like I said, it looks like I was the fool.' Facing me, he added: 'Your horse will be here within the hour, and you'll see all is well with him.'

He was about to leave – yet on impulse, I stayed him.

'What was your quarrel with Thomas Peck, the night he died?' I asked sharply – causing him to give a start.

'It was nothing,' he muttered. 'We'd taken too much drink...'

'No, there's more,' I said, summoning my magistrate's tone. 'As a forester, he was angry at you foundry men... you are a foundryman, are you not?'

Combes was looking uncomfortable now. So with my sword still levelled, and one eye on Henry Hawes, I pressed him.

'You left before Peck and I did,' I said. 'And a short time later he was dead... while someone dealt me a blow to the skull, telling me to leave Lydney. Do you know aught of that?'

No answer came. Instead, Combes allowed his gaze to shift towards the host of The Comfort – whereupon I stiffened.

'Good God, was it you? Or was it someone known to you?'

In anger I twitched the rapier, bringing it closer to Hawes's throat. Instinctively he flinched away - but I caught the look in his eye, and knew I had struck on something.

'Get up,' I snapped. 'And walk slowly before me, back into the inn.' Turning to Combes, I jerked my head towards the door. 'Bring my horse here, now – and I swear, if there's any sign of distress about him, you will suffer for it. More, you can forget about a gratuity until I'm satisfied you're guilty of nothing worse than a brabble at the inn. Do you see?'

He met my eye, but said nothing. Instead he got himself outside, while I turned my attention to the man who was now my prisoner. 'So, you're known as one of Mountford's lackeys, Master Hawes,' I said, keeping the rapier levelled. 'I somehow thought that might be the case... shall we proceed?'

\*\*\*

It was a very different interrogation from the last one I had conducted, in the castle at Gloucester, of the Spaniard Sebastien who went as a Turk. Hawes was a slippery fellow, but he was caught and he knew it. Once I had given some details to Parry, the sergeant and I took him upstairs to my old chamber. He took the only stool, while the two of us sat down on the bed. Below us, the inn remained quiet.

Being somewhat short of patience now, I went on the attack.

'Who killed Peck?' I demanded. 'Was it you?'

'Good Christ...' Hawes shook his head quickly. 'I swear on my daughter's life, I did not. Besides, you saw me go back into the inn – how could I have followed him without your knowing?'

'And yet you were evasive about his death,' I retorted. 'You knew full well he hadn't fallen and cracked his head.'

He hesitated, then: 'I still swear I would never have harmed him. He was a customer.'

'Then if not you, who did?' I threw back.

He lowered his gaze, wetting his lips: what a contrast there was now, from the stone-faced host who had seen me off, the day I left for Bristol. But Hawes had served Parry and his constables with his own hands a few hours since, and knew well enough what case he was in. Finally he swallowed, and spoke.

'I may know some things... things of value to you.'

I exchanged looks with the sergeant, but remained silent.

'You must understand...' The Comfort's host paused, looking away. 'Matters are not as you think, here in the forest. They're poor folk... miners, foundrymen and foresters, who scratch a living. When money is offered for private services – more than a man makes in a month or even a year, it's hard to say no-'

'What's this, a sermon or a history lesson?' Parry broke in. 'Master Belstrang asked you a question, so answer it.'

'You mean, as to who killed Tom Peck?' Hawes shook his head again. 'I swear I cannot tell you. You need to-'

'Damn you, Hawes,' I broke in angrily. 'Don't tell me what I need. You said you knew things of value – so out with them!'

But he was torn; both Parry and I saw it. Torn between the consequences of what he had done in the matter of Leucippus, and what might befall him if he accused someone of murder. Hence, we gave him a moment to reflect, until:

'There's a man they use, to deal with anyone who makes difficulties for them,' he said, speaking low. 'I mean the Mountfords... or I should say, Master Francis. I swear to God I don't know who he is, save that he must dwell close by. And in truth I'm glad I don't - for should I give him away, I'd likely end up in a coffin myself.'

He looked up, eying each of us in turn, and added: 'You see the power the ironmasters have - over me, and everyone else. I owe my living to them. And those who do their bidding wield power too... especially Tobias Russell. It's him you should ask – though you'll have to rack him for an answer.'

And with that, Hawes drew a breath and rose to his feet. I would have protested – but Parry laid a hand on my arm.

'I think we have enough for the present, sir, don't you?' he murmured. 'We know where Master Hawes is, if we need him again.' To the other he said: 'You have an inn to keep, don't you?'

Hawes gave the sergeant a bleak look: he was spent, his shoulders hunched. Without a word, he went to the door and left us. After a moment, I too stood up.

'Well now, it seems Francis Mountford employs an assassin,' I said. 'One who disposes of loose-tongued people who threaten his affairs. People like Thomas Peck, for example - or perhaps meddlesome men like me.' Turning the matter over, I heaved a sigh; I was indeed, I reflected once again, lucky to be alive. Facing Parry, I asked him if he believed what Hawes had said, and received a nod in reply.

'I do, sir… for he's in our power,' he said. 'Were we to charge him with horse-sealing, he could face the gallows.' He thought for a moment, then: 'It seems that a great deal rests on our apprehending your friend Master Russell in the morning – are you prepared for it?'

'I am,' I replied, after a moment. 'More, I believe I might even relish it.'

## TWELVE

We left Lydney a little after daybreak as Parry had intended, riding in quiet fashion up the river towards Cricklepit. The village was already stirring, and the foundrymen would be at work, for the furnaces are never allowed to grow cold. Our party was unchanged in every respect, save one: that the sergeant was now in possession of the bare facts concerning Russell's private shipments of ordnance.

The previous night, after what had transpired, I found it difficult to keep Parry in the dark about the true purpose behind our mission. I trusted him, and believed he could take whatever decisions were needed. Hence, we had talked for a half hour outside the inn, Parry smoking his pipe while I told my tale. In truth, I may have been somewhat loose-tongued: I was in a far better humour, for Leucippus was now back in the stable, unharmed; it was a joyful reunion. Standing under the starlit sky, I gave the sergeant a brief summary of what I knew. As he took it in, I found my gaze wandering upwards, to where the Great Comet still blazed; it was fainter now, perhaps further off.

'By God, sir…' Parry took his pipe from his mouth, and exhaled. 'I wish Justice March had told me this, before we set out. I'd have brought more men with me.'

'I believe we'll be adequate to the task,' I replied.

'We'll have to be. As you've said, it's a matter of treason - far beyond the warrants I've been given.'

'I know,' I said. 'But I'm not without powers. Give me Russell, unarmed and guarded, and I'll do the rest.'

Now, reflecting on our conversation in the cool of the morning, I wondered briefly whether I had done aright: Parry was taut, and seeing his humour his constables were silent. Yet they carried poniards and horse-pistols, and the sergeant himself was permitted to bear a sword. Between us I felt sure we could deal with any threat. As for Russell... I recalled the man's cold stare the last time we spoke, and girded myself.

We were at Cricklepit soon enough, where all appeared as normal, with the mill-wheel turning and chimneys smoking. Having dismounted as planned, we walked in a line towards the furnace-house. Soon a workman appeared, then another, to stop in alarm at the sight of armed men approaching. As we drew closer, one of them turned and called to his fellows within. I looked to Parry, who to my relief remained calm.

'Is he one of those men?' he asked me. And when I shook my head, he called aloud for Tobias Russell to show himself. But instead, the remaining foundrymen emerged from the building, to stand in a silent group.

'Where is the master?' Parry strode forward, the rest of us close behind. At sight of pistols the Cricklepit men drew back, until one was bold enough to give answer.

'He's not here,' he said, spreading his hands.

'Is that so? Well, we'll make a search,' the sergeant said. 'But when I find him – which I will do, if it takes me a week - I'll arrest you for impeding an officer of the law.' And when the man blinked in alarm, he added: 'It means I'd have to take you back with me to Gloucester. A long journey... and a long time to be away from your work, and your family.'

The foundryman swallowed, glancing at the constables – whereupon his gaze fell upon me, at which he stiffened.

'You remember me?' I said, taking a step forward to stand beside Parry. 'I've business with Master Russell again – though of a different nature.'

But my thoughts were racing. Russell, of course, would have had news of our arrival: the man had eyes in Lydney and everywhere else within miles. Had he fled, or was he merely staying out of sight? I spoke briefly to Parry, who gave no reaction. Instead, signalling to me to stay back, he drew close to the foundryman and, to my surprise, put an arm about his shoulder. Soon he had drawn him aside, the two of them speaking low. Finally he sent the man back to his fellows with a friendly slap on the back, and rejoined the rest of us.

'Russell's away,' he announced. 'But I know where he is.'

'Well, that was neatly done,' I said. 'How did you get him to talk so readily?'

Parry wore a wry look. 'I told him no charge would be brought against him, or any of the other men. There might even be a reward – you, a former justice, would petition the Mountfords for it. And I told him that if he gave me the intelligence I needed, he would be made foundry-master. His name's Lowman – I told him he'd not be such a low man after Russell was taken.'

'I'm impressed,' I said, putting on a wry look of my own. 'Though I may not be able to produce the reward you've promised, let alone see Master Lowman promoted.'

'I'll leave that to you, sir,' Parry returned. 'Now let's attend to the business in hand, shall we?'

'Gladly,' I said. 'So, where will we find Russell?'

'It's not far, my informant says,' came the answer. 'He's at a small foundry upriver, owned by one Jonas Willett... do you know it?'

\*\*\*

This time, our approach took on a very different character. Leading the horses, we walked upriver until we reached the Newerne stream. Parry then ordered the mounts to be tethered whereupon, having taken directions from me, the party advanced cautiously along the woodland path. For some reason I heard no sounds of axes that morning, which made me even more watchful; it was as if the entire forest knew of our presence.

Moreover, I was mighty puzzled. Jonas Willett was no friend of Russell... I well recalled his surly remarks, when I had

treated him and his son at The Comfort. It seemed most unlikely
that Russell would take refuge at the Willett foundry... hence,
could we be certain that the man Lowman had spoken the truth?
Was it merely evasion, a delaying tactic to allow his master to
escape? Russell must have guessed that a substantial arresting
party would not be sent without cause - and likely feared that
his own liberty was under threat.

The answers to those questions would come soon enough –
yet in ways that confound me as I recall the matter. After many
years on the magistrate's bench, I believed I could tell truth
from falsehood: now I see that a man must learn, to the very end
of his days. But I leap ahead, and will return to the little foundry
on the rushing Newerne stream, run by the hard-pressed Jonas
Willett and his son Peter.

At first, all was calm. We had seen smoke rising from the
chimney for some time, and I was unsurprised to find an air of
normality. No-one was in sight, but Parry ordered the constables
to fan out, alert for any movement. There was none, however,
until we neared the doors of the furnace house where the
sergeant called a halt. His hand was on his sword-hilt, as was
mine; all of us looked about warily - then tensed as a figure
familiar to me came out of the building, and stopped in his
tracks.

'Master Willett,' I said, with a glance at Parry. 'I find this
reunion very different to the one I expected.'

Jonas Willett stared, with a look of mingled surprise and
alarm, but made no reply - whereupon Parry moved forward.

'I hold a warrant for the arrest of one Tobias Russell,' he said,
and produced a paper from his jerkin. 'I'm given to understand
he is here.' He waited while the other took in the tidings.
Meanwhile I peered past him at the furnace-house, but saw no
movement.

'I don't understand,' Willett said, somewhat angrily. 'Why

would he be here? I have no dealings with the Cricklepit men.'

'Though you once worked for them,' I reminded him, taking a step forward, at which a frown appeared.

'You will recall that I left there, years ago,' came the retort. 'And I pray you, what business is this of yours?'

'Master Willett, you'll not question us,' Parry said. 'If the man I seek is here you must give him up, or face a charge of aiding a felon.'

'Felon?' Willett echoed. 'Nay, I'd never do such!'

But he was afraid, and everyone saw it. On impulse I looked about pointedly, then asked him where his son Peter was.

'He's somewhere about... why do you ask me that?'

'Then call him.'

Parry stepped closer to Willett, and following his lead the constables pressed forward. Finding himself hemmed in by a semi-circle of armed men, even the stout foundryman flinched.

'See now, Peter isn't here,' he said quickly. 'But given time I can fetch him, and he'll answer any questions you put... we've done no wrong.' He nodded at me. 'That man will vouch for us – we're simple working folk, is all we are...'

Yet he faltered again, aware that both Parry and I were watching him keenly. At the back of my mind, suspicions began to grow... but I was diverted by the sergeant drawing his sword.

'I think you can take us to Russell,' he said, in a cold voice: the patient sergeant had lost patience. A moment passed before, to my surprise, Willett heaved a great sigh.

'You played fast and loose with me, sir,' he said, looking hard at me. 'Using a false name and all... like I told you, my boy knew you for a snooper. What is it drives you – a reward, for hunting men down?'

There was bitterness in his voice, but there was something else too. It sounded like an overwhelming sadness.

'Justice is my reward,' I answered, somewhat sharply. 'That, and the wish to help a friend whose brother died here. And I don't believe he was crushed by a tree - indeed, I believe it's you who have played fast and loose with me!'

And I would have said more, had I not caught Parry's look. 'There'll be time for recriminations, sir,' he said. 'Let's catch our prey first, shall we?' To Willett he added: 'Lead on now. But first, I want to know where we're going.'

'You know the way already,' Willett muttered, with a dark look in my direction. 'It's in Lydney.'

\*\*\*

It was the Willetts' own house.

It stood beyond the village, on the path to Aylburton; I would have passed it, the night I walked Thomas Peck home. It was a humble cottage, with a vegetable garden and a wood-pile. Our party was there within the half-hour, leading the horses while Jonas Willett himself walked in front with Parry. He was not yet a prisoner, though few would have guessed it, the way he was guarded. As we passed through Lydney people stopped to stare, but the foundryman himself look neither to left nor right. When we reached the house, he stopped, his eyes on the ground.

'We'll follow you in,' Parry said, gesturing to the door.

But Willet held back. 'It isn't locked,' he muttered. 'You may enter as you please.'

I watched him, then threw a glance at Parry: the man was stalling. Without another word, the sergeant strode to the door. As he threw it open he called to the constables, ordering two men to cover the rear of the house, then went inside. His men hurried to obey, while I looked at the upper windows, half-covered by sagging thatch. There was no sign of movement - until the peace was shattered abruptly, by the loud crack of a pistol-shot.

It came from within the house. At once I drew my sword and started for the door, but the two remaining constables were quicker, pushing past me in their haste. Soon we were all in the hallway, calling out Parry's name. Doors banged open, boots thundered on bare floorboards... but I stayed back, one eye on the narrow staircase – and drew a sharp breath as a figure loomed above me, a smoking pistol in his hand.

Tobias Russell.

We stared at each other, until with an oath Russell turned sharply and disappeared. There was some commotion overhead, even as both constables appeared from separate doorways.

'Upstairs,' I snapped. 'I fear the sergeant's been shot.'

They ran up the stairs while I followed, heart in mouth as to what I might find. Loud voices sounded, along with the sound of a scuffle, then of someone falling over. I gained the stairhead, finding myself in a bed-chamber which took up the entire upper floor – and stopped.

My first reaction was of alarm: there was blood on the floor. But it quickly turned to one of relief, that Parry was apparently unharmed. He stood with his back to me, looking down at a figure hunched in a corner. Beside him stood his constables, pointing their firearms. As I came up, somewhat out of breath, the sergeant turned to me, then nodded towards the man who was now their captive.

I had assumed it was Russell – but it was Peter Willett.

'The pistol-shot,' I exclaimed in confusion. 'I thought...'

'He missed me, thanks be to God,' Parry replied, sounding breathless himself. 'What's worse, I lost him...' he pointed to an open window at the back. 'The varlet got out.'

And even as I turned to look there came shouts from outside, from the rear of the house. At once, Parry grasped the shoulder of the nearest constable and gave him a shove.

'After him, both of you,' he ordered. 'And fire no shots - I want him alive.'

His men ran to do his bidding, whereupon I at last turned my attention to the sprawled figure of Peter Willett... and found myself frowning. This was not the young man I had last seen at the inn, talking in animated fashion of falconets and minions: he appeared as a stranger, pale and taut, looking balefully up at the sergeant.

'Of course he missed you, dimwit,' he said harshly. 'The bullet was meant for me!'

He shifted suddenly, wincing with pain, and his eyes went downwards. Following his gaze, I saw a red stain beneath his armpit, soaking through his rough shirt.

'And by the Christ, you'll have your hands full if you catch that one,' Peter breathed.

He meant Russell... my mind whirling, I looked at Parry.'What in God's name happened?' I asked.

'I think you can guess,' came the reply. 'They were hiding Russell... mayhap until he could get clear.'

He took a breath, then frowned at his prisoner. 'It's all coming apart for you, fellow,' he said. 'But first I'll have your wound treated... I want you in better shape, to tell your tale.' To me he said: 'Your foundry-master's a desperate sort, right enough. Threw his man to the wolves, once he saw he was about to be caught. But he can't get far... unless there's another bolthole he uses.'

I made no reply; in truth, I was speechless. Now I saw it, as if a mist had cleared - to reveal not sunlight, but a darker cloud beyond. Ideas that had soared freely came into focus and settled - for I had recognised the voice of my assailant, on the night Thomas Peck had been killed.

'It was you who attacked me,' I said to Peter Willett. 'As it was you who killed Peck...'

I trailed off: the young man's eyes had closed, and his breathing slowed. In consternation, I turned to the sergeant.

'I doubt there's a surgeon in this backwater,' he said. 'But there might be a healing-woman… will you help me get him on to a bed?'

I nodded, still gazing in disbelief at the fair young man: a most unlikely assassin. Here, I knew, was the one Henry Hawes had spoken of… the one Francis Mountford used to despatch anyone who threatened his business; who must live close by, the landlord had said…

And yet the matter was far from over. Russell was at large, as I would learn soon enough: the fugitive had squeezed through the window and leaped to the ground, at the very feet of Parry's constables. But to their shame, he was a match for them: he had downed one, then used the butt of his pistol to break the head of another, before vaulting a fence and running off into the forest.

In the meantime, however, Jonas Willett and his son were in custody, facing a bleak future. And provided the younger man was able to talk, I vowed privately to draw every last scrap of intelligence from the two of them, before choosing my next course of action.

For the biggest question of all remained, as to the identities of the true begetters of the treason; the men who traded shamelessly with England's enemies.

The Concord Men.

## THIRTEEN

The following afternoon – a Friday - Parry and I questioned the prisoners in their own home.

It had been a tense thirty hours, but the time was not wasted. Parry had raised a hue and cry, and half the inhabitants of Lydney were now scouring the countryside for the fugitive Tobias Russell, led by two of his constables. A third constable was laid up at his billet, recovering from a severe blow to the head. The fourth man was with us, keeping close guard over Jonas Willett and his son.

Peter Willett's wound had been cleaned and bandaged by a village woman; fortunately for him, the pistol-ball had passed through flesh, grazing a rib but not causing mortal harm. He had lost much blood, but after taking some physic and resting he was able to talk. Not that he was willing, any more than was his father, now shrunken with fear and bitterness. The two of them sat in the parlour of their home, sullen and silent; or rather Jonas sat, while his son lay on a pallet propped up with pillows. Not a word had passed between them the entire night, Parry's constable swore. When the sergeant and I entered, both men refused to look at us - but we were ready.

'I advise you to tell all you know,' Parry said, without preamble. He found a stool and pulled it up, close enough to make both men tense. I, on the other hand, chose to stand.

'The charge will be murder of one Thomas Peck, a forester,' the sergeant added, fixing Peter Willett with a hard stare. 'Master Belstrang is of the opinion that it was you who attacked him, on a Sabbath evening twelve days ago. You then clubbed Peck to death. This, he believes, was on the orders of Tobias Russell, who will face grave charges once he's found. Do you have aught to say to that?'

No answer came, which was of small surprise to me.

'Let me spell it out,' Parry said patiently. 'If you refuse to give testimony, you will both be taken to Gloucester castle, where the keeper is well-versed in getting men to talk. His methods have caused concern in some quarters... yet he gets results.'

At that Jonas Willett stirred, but his son did not respond. Whereupon Parry looked deliberately at each of them, before settling on Peter. 'Loyalty's a fine thing,' he said. 'But somewhat misplaced in this case, wouldn't you say? Russell was prepared to sacrifice you to save his own neck - and to stop you from talking. Do you truly intend to remain silent, for his sake?'

Another moment passed – then I saw it: the older man looked near the end of his tether. The next moment, he let out a great sigh and banged a fist down on his knee.

'By the Christ... it's all up, can't you see?'

He almost spat the words out, turning upon his son. 'Tell them what they want to hear, and be done with it!' He cried. 'Plead our condition and cry mercy – for the Lord's sake, can't you do that for me, if not for yourself?'

There was desperation in his voice and in his gaze. But his son merely glowered, eyes averted.

'Your father is right,' Sergeant Parry said to him. 'Your only hope is to make a confession. Though I'll not lie to you: whatever the condition he speaks of, it makes no difference to your sentence: I have no doubt that you'll hang. Yet it's possible you can spare your father the same fate.'

'Me?' Jonas Willett swung his gaze to Parry. 'What charge do I face? Aside from telling a few untruths, perhaps-'

'Stop your gabbling!'

The words flew from Peter Willet's mouth, as he turned suddenly to his father. The movement caused him to grunt with pain, yet his eyes blazed with anger. Lifting a hand weakly, he jabbed it in the air.

'You worthless old wretch!' he breathed. 'You've always seen what you wanted to see – or dulled your wits with drink. And whose money is it, I ask, that pays for your getting soused night after night? I could...'

With an oath he broke off, gazing down at his lap. But at last, here was an opening for ex-Justice Belstrang. A notion had been surfacing, and I lost no time in voicing it.

'Foundry-work is indeed a hard life, is it not?' I said to Jonas. 'Dirty, hot and perilous - you told me so yourself, do you recall? Just the two of you, toiling every hour of daylight, doing the work of three or four men.' I paused, then: 'Few would pass up the chance to earn money elsewhere, when offered - more money, someone hereabouts told me, than a man might make in a month or even a year. Is it not so?'

But the old man merely shook his head. In a single day he had aged; he looked haggard, even close to tears. For a moment I almost sympathised with him: a widower, I had learned by now, who had struggled to bring up his child unaided... whereupon a notion soared, that struck me like a blow.

'John Mountford,' I said, turning to Peter. 'By heaven, it was you who slew him.'

A deathly silence fell. Parry's constable, standing by the doorway, tensed visibly; even the sergeant looked surprised. But I kept my gaze on the younger Willett, who refused to meet my eye... whereupon his father alarmed everyone by letting out a howl of anguish.

'No... no, he wouldn't!' he cried. 'He found the body, is all - he swore to me! Mountford was talking with some foresters - Peck, and other men. He was careless, he walked where he shouldn't have... a great elm fell on him, crushed him like a fly!' In anguish, he turned to his son. 'You swore to me! You know you did-'

'Be quiet, damn you!' Peter Willett's command - for it was

nothing less - cut his father off in an instant. But it was too late: Parry saw it, as did I. Drawing a breath, the sergeant threw me a glance, then eyed the culprit keenly.

'Is that why Thomas Peck had to die too?' He asked quietly. 'Because he talked to John Mountford, mayhap told him things you didn't want known? Or was it only after he spoke with Master Belstrang here, that you decided his life had to be snuffed out?'

Another silence followed, broken only by the older man's breaking into tears. Shaking his head, he sobbed into his beard, no longer able to look at his son... but Peter Willett shot a savage glance at him, then up at me.

'I should have cracked your skull open when I had the chance,' he muttered. 'Just as that damned fool Spry should have dealt with you...' he looked aside, then eyed Parry.

'Do what you will,' he breathed, wincing as his wound pained him. 'For it seems I'm tried and convicted already... I curse you and your whoreson castle-keeper. God knows I'll be glad to get clear of this village, and all its week-kneed grubbers. Slaves, the lot of them - like you!'

The last phrase was thrown at Jonas, who merely quailed. He was broken: a different man to the one who had blocked my way in The Comfort that night, and asked me my business. I turned away, but it seemed Peter Willett was not done yet.

'You've played the innocent dupe long enough!' he said to his father, every word thrown like a barb. 'You knew what I did, or some of what I did. You cursed the Mountfords while you served them – and you serve them still! For you know in your heart whence came the money to set up the foundry... you knew I lied about the loan, for who would loan money to a family like ours? And if part of the bargain was my serving Francis in ways you wouldn't like, you chose not to ask! By the Christ, you're as guilty as me!'

117

With that he fell silent, his mouth a hard line. It was confession enough… drawing a breath, I spoke up.

'So you killed John Mountford, because he learned of his nephew's secret business, and meaned to put an end to it,' I said, as calmly as I could. 'That's why it was bruited that his body was so ruined, his brother should not view it, for it would cause him too much distress. And I'll wager Captain Spry, who took the corpse upriver, knew what was done.' I paused, then: 'Did Mountford die as Peck did, from a mere blow to the skull?'

But Willett did not answer; indeed, he ignored me utterly. He had retreated into some part of himself, letting it be known that he would say nothing further. I turned to Parry, who was nodding.

'It matters not how the victim died,' he said. 'We have his killer… and it seems his orders came not from Russell, but directly from Russell's master: the foundry owner and paymaster, Francis Mountford himself.'

He thought for a moment, then: 'In truth, sir, I'm glad the business of charging that gentleman is somewhat beyond my rank… a matter for you and Justice March, perhaps, when we get back to Gloucester.' He eyed both Willetts: the silent son, his face a blank, and the grief-stricken father. 'And I too will be glad to get clear of this place,' he added. 'It's beginning to fill me with gloom.'

'Wait…' on impulse I lifted a hand, and looked down at Jonas. 'What did you mean, when you said Peter should plead your condition?' I asked. 'Is there something yet untold? For I advise you to tell of it, if you harbour any hope not to share your son's fate. Speak now!'

'Share his fate?' Jonas echoed bitterly. 'Why, there's precious little difference. It's but a matter of which of us dies first, and in how much pain.' Seeing neither Parry nor I understood, he tapped his head.

'They say it's a kind of a worm, in here. Though they cannot know what it's like. It's more like a scorpion - a malevolent creature, that eats at me. A chirurgeon told me, in Stroud - and charged me for the news, as if I should be grateful.' He sighed, then: 'It makes my head spin, does the scorpion… and it stings like the very devil. My only remedy against it is to pickle my brains - do you wonder at that?'

He fell silent as Parry and I gazed at him… and at last, I saw the whole picture. Since there was little more to be said, the sergeant got heavily to his feet. He left his constable to stand guard and walked to the door, and I followed.

Only when we got ourselves outside did I remember that I had not asked about the Concord Men. But I knew one name already: that of Francis Mountford.

The return to Gloucester, and then to Upton, loomed ahead; just then I was unsure whether I relished it or dreaded it. However, I had no urge to leave Lydney just yet. Two men had to be apprehended, both of whom I was eager to see caught: Tobias Russell and his trow-master, Captain Spry.

***

Night fell, and the parties returned empty-handed: Russell was still at large. But there was a different air about the village. For one thing the inn was busy, Henry Hawes and his daughter moving briskly among the drinkers. Parry and I sat in what had become my usual corner, along with one of his constables; the others guarded the Willetts' house, where father and son remained prisoners. We had taken supper, but were dispirited. Our fear was that Russell was deep in the forest, where a man could search in vain for many days.

'If he isn't found, I can't wait much longer,' the sergeant said. 'I have a murderer to escort to Gloucester, and that must satisfy Justice March. As for the father…' he let out a sigh. 'I've no stomach for dragging him with us – who would? He's a dying man.'

I had no argument with that, yet I was filled with disappointment; I had an urge to see Russell face trial for his treachery. As for Captain Spry: he could deny all knowledge of the actions of my assailant Yakup. Yet I had witnessed his behaviour at Bristol, and knew he was aware of where the Mountford cannons were bound. In some ways, I was as eager to see him charged as I was Russell.

I was about to make some remark to Parry, when a figure pushed his way through the throng and stood before us. Looking up, I was surprised to meet the eye of Combes, the ruffian who had almost bought Leucippus.

'I would speak with you,' he muttered. 'On business.'

Parry peered at the man, then turned to me with an enquiring look. 'Someone else you know, sir?'

I nodded, not wanting to elaborate. 'If you seek the gratuity I spoke of, for returning my horse,' I began – but Combes shook his head.

'Not that.' He leaned forward like a stage conspirator, then spoke low: 'I can take you to Russell.'

'Can you, now?' Parry frowned at him. 'Why would you? Is it a reward you seek, or...?'

'Does it matter?' The other glanced about to satisfy himself he was not overheard, then faced me. 'I played fair with you, master, did I not? Treated your horse well, and brought him back?' He paused, then: 'You know I was duped by that bastard Hawes – I've no quarrel with you. Even if you suspected me of killing Peck, when all I did was fight him-'

'There's no need to remind me,' I said, somewhat sharply. 'Why not make your offer and be done?'

Combes hesitated, glancing at a vacant stool, whereupon Parry gave a sigh and nodded. At once the man sat down, his bulky form filling the small table. 'I can take you there this very night,' he murmured. 'And my price is five sovereigns.'

'Is it, indeed?' Parry threw the would-be informant a scathing look. 'You must dwell in cloud-cuckoo-land, friend. More, I don't like you. I've half a mind to arrest you, if I can come up with a charge-'

'The charge would be affray,' I said at once. 'Master Combes is a familiar face hereabouts... he knows what I speak of.'

Yet, despite my tone, I felt a pang of excitement. Combes would hardly make such an offer without being able to deliver... I glanced at Parry, and caught his eye.

'Well then, why not simply tell me where to find Russell?' he asked, after a moment. 'I'll give you two shillings: one in advance, and the other when we apprehend the fugitive.'

'Shillings, is it?' At that, the other grew angry. 'You think I'm a fool? You could blunder about for weeks here and not find your man - and I swear no-one else will come to you as I've done. Frightened rabbits, most of them. Besides, if I told you, you'd likely go off without paying me a farthing!'

A moment passed, but Parry looked as if he would refuse to budge: a stubbornness was upon him. Was our quarry to escape justice, I wondered, now that the sergeant had a murderer in custody?

On a sudden, there seemed only one solution.

'I'll pay you two sovereigns,' I said to Combes, causing all three heads to turn towards me. 'The first now, the other when we've got Russell.'

'Master Belstrang, I wouldn't advise...' Sergeant Parry began, but he was cut short.

'Agreed,' Combes snapped. 'And I want my name left out. I came to you to get the money you promised me, after I was duped in the matter of your horse. You paid me a groat for feeding him, then I asked when you were leaving. That's what I'll say to any nosy varlet that asks – does it suit?'

I hesitated; Parry looked disapproving, but did not gainsay me. Only when I gave Combes a nod did he speak up.

'It's your money, sir, when all's said and sifted. And if that's how it's to be...' he gave a shrug, then eyed Combes again. 'But I want to know which direction we're going in. Nor do I want to move now – it's too easy to lose a man in the dark. We'll leave at first light – provided you swear Russell will remain where you say he is.'

To this Combes nodded quickly; he was edgy, and ready to make himself scarce. 'I'll await you on the road, at sunup, east of the village,' he said. 'There I'll take my sovereign. Once I've guided you, I'll take the other. After that I'm gone, and you'll not ask after me again.' But as he began to rise from the table, Parry stayed him.

'One moment... east, you say? Where are we bound?'

'For Purton,' came the hurried reply – whereupon Parry's constable, who had been frowning at the man, put out a hand to grasp Combes's arm.

'We've already searched there,' he said harshly. 'One of the first places we looked... do you think we're dupes, like you?'

At that Combes's eyes flashed. Turning angrily to the man, he wrenched his arm away, causing the other to rise. For a moment it looked as if another affray was about to erupt... but thankfully, it was averted.

'You looked, you say?' Combes sank down on to his stool again, mastering himself. 'Mayhap you did, but did you search every last cranny? Would you even know where to begin?'

The constable paused, then sat down. Whereupon in some relief, I faced Parry again.

'It's his only escape route, all things considered,' I ventured. 'He can't hide in the forest for ever. He's waiting until the next trow sails... once he gets to Bristol, he's away.' I pondered the matter, then: 'It's clear he's given up his life here. He knows it's the last throw of the dice... he's armed, and he's desperate.'

'And yet, this man seems to have known all along where he was,' Parry said, looking hard at Combes. 'How is that?'

On a sudden, I stiffened: a silence had fallen across the inn, with all eyes turned in our direction. In the corner beside the barrels, Henry Hawes stood stock-still. Everyone seemed to be waiting - then I caught the look of alarm in Combes's eyes, and understood.

'Away with you!' I said loudly, rising swiftly and placing a hand on my sword. 'I could arrest you for making threats! We'll leave when we're good and ready, and not before! Do you understand?'

Whereupon, amid the consternation that followed, I leaned close to Combes's ear. 'Daybreak, as arranged,' I hissed. 'Or I'll put it about that you informed on the Willetts.'

With that I drew back, eying the man as he got to his feet. Hiding his relief at my action, he threw a scowl at the three of us and lurched away, shoving drinkers aside in his apparent anger.

Even the unlikeliest of men, I often find, can play-act most convincingly when they must.

## FOURTEEN

The morning was chill; September was waning now, and a scent of autumn pervaded the air as our party set forth. Not wishing to attract attention, we were on foot and in pairs: Parry and myself leaving first, then two of his constables a short while later. A half mile to the east, well clear of the village, we gathered to await our guide; a tense, alert group. Mercifully it was not long before Combes, in a hat pulled low, stepped out of the trees that lined the road.

As agreed, I paid the man, who took his fee without a word. Nothing was said as we started towards Purton at a good pace, until after a while Combes halted. Almost hidden in the haze coming off the river, a path sloped away to our right.

'Why do you stop?' Parry asked. 'We're not at the quay.'

'That's true enough,' Combes replied. 'And nor is Russell.'

As one, we turned sharply to him: to say that no-one present trusted this man would be well short of the mark. Seemingly unconcerned, however, he pointed.

'The salt-marshes... few go down there, save fisher-folk. You'll need to watch your step, masters.' He wore a sour grin, which put Parry's back up.

'It's you who need watch your step,' he retorted. 'For you're going to walk in front. Did you think to leave us floundering in a bog?'

'I did not,' Combes said. 'You must follow in my footsteps in any case, for I know the safe paths. You'll see the hut soon enough, but you won't be able to get near it without me.'

The four us eyed him, before I voiced the suspicions of all. 'You're telling us that Russell's hiding there in plain view? Why is he not by the quay, ready to take a boat?'

'Because he knows you'd expect it,' Combes said. 'He's not a fool. I'll wager he's already got word to Spry or some other trow-master to drop anchor soon, as close to shore as they can. He swims like an eel, does Russell. Since he was a boy.'

He waited, with growing impatience, but Parry wasn't done.

'How can you be sure he's there?' he demanded – to which the reply came as something of a shock.

'Because I took him. It's my hut… and don't ask what I use it for. Now are you ready, or are you not?'

In stunned silence, we gazed at him. I've met some rogues in my time, but few were as devoid of shame as Combes: a varlet who would have sold his own children into slavery if he had any. He was a smuggler, a thief and probably worse, but just then there was no time for scruples. With a sigh, Parry gave the man a curt nod. Thereafter we left the Lydney road and walked south-east, the land falling away towards the mighty Severn.

It was but a short walk before the flat marshland appeared: salt-water pools amid clumps of coarse grass, and not a tree or bush to break the melancholy view. Wading birds took flight at our approach, gulls shrieked, and the ground quickly became treacherous. Soon we were obliged to walk in single file while Combes – the marsh-rat, I would dub him later – led the way.

And almost at once, we saw the hut.

It was tiny: a rough-bult hovel squatting on the marsh, its roof of reeds crudely thatched. It was no more than a hundred yards off, yet it might have been miles, for between it and our party lay a morass of soggy turf interlaced with channels. Beyond the hut the marshes petered out, giving way to the river's shore. It would indeed be possible to reach a boat, I saw - provided you were prepared to get wet and muddy.

'But he'll see us, long before we see him.'

Parry's leading constable, the older of the two and the one who had challenged Combes in the inn, was uneasy. Squinting ahead, the sergeant tensed, but at once Combes spoke up.

'There are no windows,' he grunted. 'It's not a house, nor was it built for comfort. Stay low, follow me and keep your mouths shut, is all you need do. He isn't expecting me, or I would have signalled with a call. When we're close enough to see the path to the hut, I'm leaving you... though not before I get the rest of my money.'

He was looking at me – but at once Parry turned upon him.

'You're not leaving until I have Russell,' he snapped. 'That was the bargain... and how would we find our way back? You won't see another penny until you guide us to firm ground.'

There followed a taut moment, which could have become a stalemate. Combes tensed like a bullock, but what choice had he? Both constables placed hands on pistol-butts, while the sergeant grasped his sword-hilt... and once again, it seemed, Justice Belstrang was obliged to play the peacemaker.

'Guide us, and stay clear while these men apprehend Russell,' I said with a sigh. 'Once he's restrained, bring us back across the marsh, then I'll pay you at once. After that you're away, and none shall know you brought us here – save Russell, I expect.'

To my relief Combes nodded, his scowl giving way to a look of resignation. But as he turned to lead on, Parry stayed him.

'Wait – do you know if the fellow's armed?'

'I'd think him a whoreson dolt if he wasn't,' came the surly reply. 'But like I told you, he's no fool.' With that, he turned away abruptly and began to tread through the mire, picking his way carefully – and seemingly not caring whether we followed or not.

It took no more than a few minutes to reach the hut.

The last yards were easier, as Combes had said: a narrow path, marked out with stakes driven deep into the soft ground. Now he was allowed to hang back, as Parry and his men closed in. The hovel stood on a slight rise: the only firm spot for a hundred yards. The entrance had to be on the far side, with a view out to the river... and the place was eerily silent.

As if by design the four of us halted. But the sergeant kept a cool head, directing one man to go around each side of the hut. First, however, pistols were made ready. Though my pulse was thudding I was eager to play a part, but with a frown Parry stayed me: this was his task, and not mine.

So with a nod I kept in the rear, one eye on Combes who was squatting on the path, looking taut and wary. The silence was broken only by the distant cries of birds - whereupon quite quickly, it was shattered. No sooner had Parry and his men disappeared round the sides of the hut, than mayhem broke out.

The first I knew, a pistol roared. It was followed by a cry, then shouts… and forgetting all notions of caution, I darted forward. In a second I had rounded the hovel, hand on sword… only to stop in horror.

Before me, the older constable lay on his back with arms thrown wide, pistol in hand and still cocked. One glance was enough: he was stone-dead, brains and blood oozing from his skull where he had been shot at close range. Beside him, crouching in fear, the younger man was aiming his firearm shakily at the doorway - from whence came muffled cries, followed by a jarring thud as someone crashed against the flimsy wall of the hut. Heart in mouth, I lurched towards the dark interior – only to be knocked flat.

For a few seconds I was winded, dimly aware of noises and of shapes moving wildly above me. Then came another pistol-shot: thinking the constable had found his target, I tried to rise… only to find that he had disappeared.

Or rather, he was sitting on the grass, I soon saw: pale and wide-eyed, staring at nothing. Forcing myself on to my rump, I would have called out - whereupon he keeled over like a puppet. Then I saw the blood, and the poniard protruding from his chest…

'Master Belstrang! For God's sake!'

I whirled about, towards the sound of Parry's voice. A few yards away, he and Tobias Russell were locked in a kind of dance, wrestling violently. The sergeant had lost both his sword and his pistol, and both men grappled for possession of his poniard. But it was clear who was the stronger: Russell, sweating and cursing, had a hand on Parry's throat. And even as I struggled to my feet, he threw a baleful glare at me.

'Keep back!' He cried. 'Or I'll slay you too!'

Breathing hard, I dragged my sword from its scabbard. A moment later I had its point pressed against his thick jerkin, while with my left hand I pulled my own poniard from my belt. Without thinking, I stabbed Russell's hand. He hissed with pain, and blood spurted, yet still he held his opponent's throat - and Parry was weakening, grasping the other's wrist. Whereupon, all I could think of was to lay the poniard against Russell's neck, across the pulsing vein, and try to sound convincing.

'Release him, or I'll slice you,' I ordered.

What followed seemed to take a minute or more, though it was only seconds. Russell tried to jerk his head away, yet I pressed my blade tighter, almost breaking the skin. Only now did I realize that the man was desperate enough to die where he stood – but mercifully, Parry seized his chance. Letting go of his assailant's wrist, he brought his hand back, made a fist and slammed it into Russell's face with all his strength.

To my heartfelt relief, the foundry-master sagged, then his knees buckled... and watched by the two of us, he sank to the ground. As I took a step away Parry stooped, brought his own dagger to Russell's throat and held it there.

'Stay down, and be still,' he breathed. 'For just now, I'd fain stick you like a pig.'

Dazed, with blood running from his shattered nose, Russell peered up at us both. Whereupon, gathering my wits, I sheathed my own poniard but levelled my sword at his chest. Panting, he looked down at the blade, then fixed me with a bleak look.

'Do it, then!' he spat. 'Finish it now... for I'm not leaving here – and you can go to the devil!'

'Well now, doubtless that would suit you,' I said, catching my breath. 'But you'll answer for your crimes according to law.' I threw a glance at Parry, relieved to see him mastering himself... until his gaze fell on the blood-soaked body of his younger constable. With a gasp, he whirled towards Russell...

I let out a cry, but too late.

As in some ghastly dream, I saw the rapid movement of Parry's dagger – a slashing stroke, which produced an immediate fountain of gore. Russell's whole body jerked... his hand went to his neck, clutching wildly, while blood welled through his fingers. In dismay – and with mingled regret, too – I staggered back, lowering my sword as the man slumped.

There on the salt marsh, the life ebbed out of him; and quite soon, Russell's was the third corpse to lie on the turf, which had begun to resemble a battlefield.

It was over. In the moment that followed sea-birds screeched, as if to condemn Sergeant Parry for what he had done. Yet, numbed as I was, one thought above all others came at once to my mind.

With Russell dead, who would tell me of The Concord Men?

\*\*\*

The rest of that day remains a farrago to me. Though one thought soon occurred, a salutary lesson: ex-Justice Belstrang was too old to be engaging in hunts for murderous fugitives, let alone armed conflict. I made a resolve: that I would wear a sword when compelled to do so for formality's sake, yet I would never draw it again, nor even my old poniard. But there will be time enough to speak of such things; in my mind's eye I see the windswept Lydney marshes and the blood-spattered grass, and the forlorn sight of Parry's two dead constables. I believe the sergeant changed then, before my eyes: racked with guilt and grief, it's said that he never smiled again, and seldom spoke.

There had been five of us, who set out on the path through the mire; now there were just three. For to my surprise Combes had kept his place, instead of turning tail at the sound of pistol-shots. Russell, of course, had fired first, I learned: alerted by the sound of someone approaching, he had shot the constable on sight. As Parry lunged at him, the man had avoided his sword and fallen back into the hut, drawing his poniard. The two then fought, which is when I appeared, only to be thrown to the ground when they careered outside. Unnerved by events, the younger constable had fired his pistol wildly and missed – and paid a terrible price. Having dealt Parry a dizzying blow, Russell had freed himself long enough to thrust his dagger into the constable's heart, before the sergeant was upon him again...

The rest I have already related; and God knows, to relive it once again is more than enough.

And so, the hard-faced foundry-master I had first encountered at Cricklepit, in my brief alias as William Pride, had succeeded in slaying two armed men before he was overpowered. It would be the talk of the Forest of Dean for years: a debacle, the likes of which had never been known.

Combes, yet in ignorance of the terrible loss of life, was chastened when he saw only Parry and myself leave the hut, mudded and grim. But he asked no questions, nor was he told what had occurred. Leaving the dead men where they lay, the sergeant and I allowed him to guide us back through the marsh. Once we stood at its edge, with the path to the Lydney road ahead, he awaited his payment in silence, prompting a bitter outburst from Parry.

'Take yourself out of my sight,' he muttered. 'For I'll be damned if you get another penny.'

Combes drew a breath, his hard gaze flitting from the sergeant to me. But sensing this was no time to protest, he lowered his eyes, let out a muffled oath and walked away.

On reflection, I believe it's the only time I have failed to keep my word. I never saw the man again, which was a small relief.

In Lydney, having walked there together in silence, Parry and I parted. He would speak with his remaining constables, and find men to recover the bodies of Russell and the others. Combes was not the only one who knew the paths through the marsh, it transpired, and for a modest payment several villagers would be engaged to undertake the grim task. For myself, my only desire was to get to The Comfort, to remove my damp clothes and rest.

When I at last walked through the door I found Henry Hawes waiting anxiously. 'I heard shots were fired, sir,' he said at once. 'Down at the marsh... has Russell been taken?'

'Russell's dead,' I told him. 'And that's all I'll say. Have some hot water sent up to my room... and a cup of sack too.'

He blinked, then turned to obey until I stayed him.

'I'll be leaving here soon. You can make up the reckoning when you please... in the meantime, you may thank God I'm forgetting what you tried to do with my horse. More, I'm choosing not to speculate as to how much you know of Francis Mountford's business. The officers and I will be gone, along with our prisoner – and in time, you'll likely see some changes hereabouts. As I said once, I have grown mighty tired of the company.'

I left him, standing at the foot of the staircase as I ascended. Once in my chamber, however, a tiredness came over me, the likes of which I have rarely known. Within minutes I was asleep, fully clothed and sprawled across the bed. I never heard Hawes's daughter when she came in with my drink. When I awoke the sun was sinking, the inn was astir below me, and a bowl of cold water stood by the bed.

Then as I rose stiffly, a notion flew to mind that made my spirits sink. I had been away from home for nigh on three weeks, and knew nothing of events. What of Thirldon, and George's efforts to petition the King... what of Hester and Childers, and the rest of my loyal household?

Would I even have a home to return to?

## FIFTEEN

The following day, the Sabbath, Parry and I made preparations to return to Worcester with our prisoner. Yet there was one matter still to be addressed: that of Captain Spry.

It was late morning before the two of us talked, standing outside the inn in the sunlight. Much had been done already, Parry's remaining constables having taken on the grim task of wrapping the bodies of their fallen comrades, to be tied on horseback and taken to their families. Russell would be buried in Lydney, by the parson of St Mary's. Parry, looking pale and taut, had barely slept, yet was resolved to see this final part of his commission through.

'I've failed already, in ways I could never have compassed,' he said. 'I do not intend to lose another quarry.'

'You and I will go to Purton together,' I told him. 'Your men have enough to do.'

It was agreed; indeed, he seemed glad of my support. Hence, a short time later we were mounted, riding the mile or so to the quay in silence. On arrival, we found a trow moored up - but it was not the *Lady Ann*. Instead, I was surprised to encounter my one-time rescuer, glum-faced Captain Darrett, standing on the quayside with other men. At sight of us he stood aside, waited for Parry and I to dismount, then came forward.

'I do hear you've been in a tussle, sir,' he murmured. 'Blood and thunder on the marshes, and men slain. Yet here you are again, and unharmed... a lucky man, I've decided.'

His greeting was warm enough, however, whereupon I made him and the sergeant known to each other. Seeing we were on business Darrett would have left us, until the name Spry was mentioned.

'Well now,' he said, 'As to that, I fear you're too late.'

'How so?' Parry asked at once.

'Spry's up and gone,' came the reply. 'Sailed two days ago in a hurry.' His doleful look, that I recalled so well, was soon in place. 'He had to make do with just one crewman, I heard... the others left him. Some dark business afoot... then, I never trusted the fellow.' He paused, then: 'What did you want him for? Was it that business of the Turk?'

But he received no answer. Parry and I exchanged looks: he had now lost the second man for whom he held a warrant. With a sigh, I glanced past the Captain to the other men on the quayside, and thought one or two of them looked familiar.

'Not that I care much,' Darrett went on. 'Though I pity the foundrymen... Cricklepit's been abandoned, did you know?' And when we both turned to him: 'They haven't been paid for weeks, and now their master's gone, they're somewhat adrift.'

He gave a sigh, then: 'I suppose there won't be any cannons to ship for a while. Strange times, eh? I still say it's due to that blasted star.' He pointed at the heavens, as if the Great Comet were somehow visible in clear blue sky.

'Do you know where Spry is gone?' Parry asked, to which Darrett gave one of his shrugs.

'From what I hear, he didn't say. Likely he'll head for Bristol, but who knows?'

'Well, to blazes with him,' I said, in a burst of anger. And yet, my disappointment was tinged with relief. There was no possibility of pursuing the errant Spry now, nor had I much desire for it. But Parry, I knew, thought differently.

'See now, it's only to be expected that the man would take flight,' I told him. 'He knew he was in peril if he stayed here. In time he may take a wrong step and be caught, yet just now you and I have more pressing business. Once my report is delivered, Justice March can decide what course to take.' I nodded towards the knot of men, who were watching us with interest. 'Do you see your informant there – Master Lowman? Perhaps it's worth your speaking to him.'

A moment passed while Parry considered my words. In truth, I saw, he was close to despair. But he gave a nod and walked off towards the group. Darrett watched him go, then eyed me.

'What became of the Turk – that villain Yakup?' He asked. 'Is he for the gallows?'

'I believe so,' I said, not wishing to pursue the topic. 'But what of you? Are you for Worcester again soon?'

'I might be,' the captain answered. 'I've a load of timber due...' he paused, then bent closer. 'I did hear talk, that there might be a different kind of cargo needs carrying upriver... somewhat more precious. Word gets round quick, you see... I had half a notion that's what you came down here for today. In which case, Master Belstrang sir, I would have to refuse. With respect, that is.'

I met his eye, and understood. 'You're mistaken,' I said. 'The cargo you speak of will be taken on horseback, escorted by the sergeant and myself. Though in truth, I'd be glad to engage you for the task before I would any other man.'

To that Darrett nodded, with his habitually melancholy face. Soon after, he and I took our farewells for what could be the last time. Though I do harbour a notion I may see the *Last Hope* one day, moored beside the quay at Worcester.

I would not go aboard, however. I believe now that I'll never view a Severn trow in the same way, ever again.

A short while later, Parry and I got ourselves mounted and took the road back to Lydney. The sergeant had spoken briefly with Master Lowman who, it transpired, had decided to forgo the promised promotion and come to the harbour to seek work, along with the other men. The foundry, now masterless, had indeed been abandoned, its furnace allowed to cool for the first time in years. There would be no cannons cast at Cricklepit for the foreseeable future - whatever their intended destination might have been.

It seemed fitting enough.

***

Early the next morning our party left Lydney, with a long day's ride ahead back to Worcester.

There had been few farewells, nor were any villagers there to see us ride out. My feelings on leaving The Comfort were mainly of relief, tinged with a foreboding of what I might find when I at last got home to Thirldon. I had used the previous evening to finish my report for March, sparing no details save one: Tobias Russell, I said, had died in a deathly struggle with Sergeant Parry, who slew him in self-defence. That dealt with, I was most restless to depart.

Henry Hawes, having taken his fee, busied himself at once and left me to carry my bag out to the stable, where Leucippus was eager to be outdoors. The boy had him saddled and readied, whereupon I lost no time in leading him out to the street. And soon, a sad little cavalcade of horsemen appeared: Parry and his constables, leading two other horses bearing the slain men, bundled and tied across the backs of their own mounts.

In the middle, on the gelding I had borrowed from Justice March, rode Peter Willett. His hands were bound before him, allowing only enough leeway to enable him to hold the reins. For good measure his thighs were laced to the stirrups; no chances would be taken to allow the man to escape. Despite his wound, he was calm and stolid.

Jonas Willett's name was all but forgotten, nor did I see him again. Later I would learn that the man had sold his foundry and retreated to his cottage, where he died soon after, in pain and grief. And as our subdued group left the village, I could not help feeling that after all that had happened, the Forest of Dean would be glad of our departure.

Yet in two respects our journey had borne fruit: if it had failed to bring back the wanted men, Tobias Russel and Captain Spry, it had at least produced John Mountford's murderer, which I hoped would afford some comfort to his brother. And more, it had succeeded in diverting this ex-magistrate's thoughts from the matter of his losing his home at the whim of our profligate monarch.

I have said elsewhere that, despite King James's titles and accomplishments - peacemaker, father of princes and author of books on kingship, tobacco and witches - I have other names for him.

Mercifully enough, the journey up to Gloucester was uneventful. We took it slowly, occasioning stares as we passed through the villages *en route*, but without stopping. Rests were taken on the open road, the horses fed and watered at streams. And all the while, Peter Willett sat his mount without a word.

In truth, I was now uncertain as to whether the man would talk, which troubled me with regard to uncovering more names: I speak of the Concord Men. It could be that Willett only knew Francis Mountford, who was unlikely to have told him more than he needed. I spoke of it to Parry in the late afternoon as we left Highnam village, with but a few miles of travel remaining. But he was uncommunicative, saying that it was a matter for Justice March, or perhaps for the keeper of the gaol. It was clear that the sergeant wished only to rid himself of his prisoner as early as possible... for which, I found, I could hardly blame him.

In silence, tired and saddle-weary, we at last entered Gloucester. On arrival I went with Parry to deliver Peter Willett to the castle, into the hands of Daniel Gwynne. It was a brief meeting: I had no desire to converse with that man, saying only that I would hand my report to the Justice. After the sergeant had supplied Gwynne with the bare details of Willett's offence, he accompanied me outside to make his farewell.

'I pray you, don't berate yourself too harshly,' I said to him. 'Though I cannot condone what you did, you might have lost your own life upon the salt-marsh, or even at the Willetts' house. More, the men we went to apprehend were, at the final throw, but small fish in the pond. Your prize – the murderer of John Mountford – is worth a deal more. He may yet be the key to the cracking open of a conspiracy, greater than either of us had imagined.'

Alas, the man was inconsolable. His task now was to take the bodies of two of his trusted men to their families. He even spoke of quitting his post thereafter. In the end we parted with a brief handshake, before I got myself mounted again and rode the short distance to Thomas March's house.

And it was there that matters took a somewhat unexpected turn, which I am eager to relate.

\*\*\*

After supper, mighty glad to feel rested and clean, I spoke at length with my host about the whole affair. He had by now read my complete report, and was confounded by it.

'Treason,' he muttered, for the third or fourth time. 'The most heinous of crimes – and committed by supposedly loyal Englishmen. In truth I have my suspicions, yet we only know one name for certain: that of Francis Mountford. Clearly he is the one to be confronted, to discover who else makes up this villainous cohort – these so-called Concord Men.' He paused, before favouring me with a wry smile. 'However, since we last met, I have not been idle.'

He went on to tell me that he had written to the High Sheriff of Gloucester as well as the Chief Justice in London, who had the ear of the King. His Majesty, in fact, was now returning from his summer progress, and Whitehall was abuzz. In short, unbeknown to me, things had begun to move. And as for the unfolding crisis in Europe…

'Frow what I hear, it's true enough that a war is building, Robert,' March said with a sigh. 'Spain is sending money to support the Archduke's troops in Bohemia. You may be aware that a number of the landowners in the Forest of Dean are papists – recusants, like old Sir Edward Wintour. He's related by marriage to the Marquis of Worcester, of Raglan Castle – and his oldest son will inherit his ironworks. Men like those may indeed be bold enough to aid the forces of the Emperor, as your Spanish informant admitted – and they're well placed to supply ordnance. But they would have to do it secretly, through lesser men like Mountford, who are prepared to take great risks for substantial reward.'

'And behind the back of his own father,' I said, with some bitterness. In my mind's eye I saw again the handsome, cool-headed man who had spoken gravely of Sir Richard's frailty, and what pains Francis and his wife took to avoid distressing him; how I would enjoy the sight of him being put in chains.

'So, it's more than a matter of mere profit for those landowners,' I said. 'They run risks themselves, but for the old cause: that of advancing Popery across Europe.'

'Indeed,' March replied. 'And many now believe this war could prove one of the gravest Europe has seen. But the Concord Men are the worst offenders here: they may not all be Papists themselves, as Mountford is not. Pure greed is their spur... a familiar enough motive, to men like you and me.'

'It's true enough,' I sighed, turning the matter over. 'And it seems imperative that someone questions Francis Mountford soon, to force him to name his fellow *Hombres de la Concordia*, as our Spanish captive called them.' I was frowning. 'At times like these, one might even think to call on the skills of a man like Daniel Gwynne.'

'Except for the fact that the Mountford seat is at Foxhill by Upton, in your home county of Worcestershire,' March said.

'It's outside my bailiwick, let alone Gwynne's.'

He was looking pointedly at me – whereupon I at once divined his meaning.

'What? How could I rack him?' I demanded, with some heat. 'I'm no longer a Justice – and he's a powerful man, who could refuse to be questioned. The High Sheriff himself needs to take the reins – I speak of Sir Samuel Sandys.'

'That's so,' March agreed. 'As is happens, I've written to him too.'

With mounting unease, I frowned at him. 'That was somewhat bold of you, sir,' I said. 'You have no warrant beyond the shire of Gloucester, while I have none at all. I'm even on bad terms with our own Justice Standish, back in Worcester.'

With gloom threatening to descend, I took a good pull from my cup of sack before setting it down heavily.

'By heaven -I wish I'd never seen Richard Mountford's letter, let alone gone to try and lift his spirits,' I said. 'For now I'm in sore need of someone to lift my own.'

At that, March couldn't help a smile appearing. 'Come now, Master ex-Justice,' he said. 'You talk as if all's lost. Your reputation has long exceeded the bounds of your county, did you not know it? I speak not of small indiscretions like keeping a common-law wife – or of your falling foul of the worthies of Worcester with your notorious stubbornness. Can you not take heart from my words?'

'And yet, just now I fail to see what more I can do.'

'But isn't it obvious?' Came the brisk reply. 'You should ride to Upton and challenge Francis Mountford to a duel. Give him the lie, so that as a gentleman he'll have no choice but to accept. Then, once he's at your mercy, you can demand he confesses all.'

I blinked – then caught the spark in the man's eye, and let out a breath. 'In God's name, sir... I would have thought this was not a time for jests - even from you!'

And yet, despite everything, a surge of laughter was threatening to bubble up inside me. To my chagrin, it occurred to me that I had not laughed aloud since that evening, almost three weeks back, when my servants Henry and Lockyer had waylaid me with their request to attend the play in Worcester. It was a relief... and hence, what could I do but embrace it?

'Enough, Master Justice,' I said at last, dabbing my eyes with a napkin. 'You cheer me, even though my predicament – and yours too, perhaps - yet remains: how to break this fearful plot and expose the Concord Men. I see no solution... do you?'

A moment passed, as we both grew solemn again. But after a moment's thought, March spoke up. 'You need to find out Francis Mountford's weakness, then play upon it for all your worth. All men have one, do they not?'

I paused... whereupon one of those notions of mine flew up. 'Well indeed, they often do,' I replied. 'And in truth, I might just know what that man's is.'

And when March raised his brows, I told him.

'I'm speaking of his wife.'

## SIXTEEN

When I left Gloucester the following day to ride back upriver to Upton, I carried a number of papers that afforded me a degree of comfort, if not of real authority. One of them was a letter from Justice March, a copy of the one he had sent to Sir Samuel Sandys, the High Sheriff of Worcester. Another was a signed confession from a Spanish prisoner in custody at Gloucester Castle, admitting to overseeing quantities of ordnance being shipped to Hamburg for conveyance to Austria. And the third was a confession from one Peter Willett of Lydney, a hired assassin who had admitted to the slaying of John Mountford, gentleman.

The confessions of course were fabrications, concocted by Daniel Gwynne. I dislike the word 'forgery', but on this occasion the cause was desperate. In truth, I knew, neither prisoner had confessed to anything, much to the impatience of their keeper. Yet, as March had assured me, those men were no longer my concern. Both would face the gallows in time, and I confess I had little sympathy for either. And when all is said, there was justice in the notion that Yakup, as I still thought of him, and Willett too, could play a role in bringing their paymasters to book. Just now, I had a far weightier matter on my mind: how to confront Francis Mountford, and get him to condemn himself.

On the long ride I had ample time to consider. The fact was, the man was guilty of treason. He had betrayed and cheated the King, as had his fellow Concord Men; and knowing what I did of James Stuart, his wrath would be sated only by seeing the harshest of penalties dealt out. The previous night, March and I had agreed on a strategy of sorts, though the outcome was in some doubt. Among other things, I feared for Sir Richard when he learned what wickedness had been done in his name, if without his knowledge – indeed, on that score, it was quite likely he may not even be believed.

It was one of the gravest predicaments I have faced. And by late afternoon, having broken my journey at Tewkesbury, I was in turmoil when I at last reached Upton and crossed the river. I could only hope I had judged aright, and that Maria Mountford might provide me with a means of getting the truth out of her husband. I see now that it was a somewhat tawdry strategy, yet I saw no other. For if Francis learned what had occurred down in the Forest of Dean, I expected that he would flee at once; what choice had he, when his life would be forfeit?

Moreover, I wondered, might he have had news already?

Troubled by these thoughts, I rode a tired Leucippus through the gates of Foxhill and drew rein in the courtyard, to find that all was tranquil. Men were at work in the nearby rose garden, a maid was gathering clean sheets from a hedge, and a lively young stable boy soon appeared to attend to my mount. I then walked heavily towards the doors of the manor, to be greeted by Mountford's servant. A short time later I was escorted to a pleasant chamber overlooking the nearby woods, where Maria Mountford herself stood up to greet me. She had been sitting with a companion, who rose and made her curtsey.

'Master Belstrang... what an unexpected pleasure.'

Mistress Mountford's voice was languid as ever... indeed, she appeared somewhat heavy-lidded and slow in her movements. With an effort I made my greetings, before asking how she fared.

'We are all well, sir... though I regret I cannot say the same for Sir Richard.' And when I tensed, she added: 'He's taken a turn for the worse, since you were last here... alas, we fear the end will not be long.'

'That's grave news,' I managed to say. 'Might I be permitted to see him?'

She appeared to consider, while avoiding my gaze. I glanced briefly at the servant: a very pretty young woman, standing with eyes downcast. A moment passed, before her mistress turned to her.

'Katherine, will you take word to my husband that a guest is come?'

As Katherine went off to obey, the lady faced me and invited me to sit close by her. Striving to appear at ease, I did so, then asked after Francis, which produced a sigh.

'Much weighed down with business, sir. The foundrymen are troublesome down in Dean. It pains me to see him so occupied.'

'Cannot Sir Richard advise him?' I asked, somewhat abruptly. 'Surely his knowledge and experience would be invaluable.'

'As I said, sir, my father-in-law is unwell,' came the reply. Was there an edge to her voice? I murmured some words of condolence.

'Very kind... now, Master Belstrang, might I enquire what brings you here? Though you are of course most welcome... was it fishing, or hunting we spoke of last time? I forget.'

My mind busy, I sought to compose an answer. Meanwhile Mistress Mountford allowed a yawn to escape, before stifling it without much effort – whereupon I blinked: I had caught the whiff of strong spirits on the woman's breath. Just then, however, footsteps sounded from the hallway, and Francis walked in. He wore a perfunctory smile of welcome... but at sight of me, it faded quickly.

'Belstrang... why, you take me by surprise, sir. I thought... but no matter.' Turning to the mistress of the house, he added quickly: 'Katherine spoke of a guest, without providing me with a name. Somewhat remiss of you, was it not?'

'Was it?' his wife answered vaguely. 'Your pardon, sir... what a silly girl I am become.'

At once there was tension in the room, which caused me some

embarrassment. And yet, I thought, might this not afford me an opening, sooner than expected? Having risen at Francis's arrival, I followed him in sitting again, girding myself for some verbal sparring. To the man's polite enquiry, which echoed his wife's, I made a reply that startled both of them.

'In truth, I come to bring news,' I said. 'But first, a confession: I did not ride here today from my estate by Worcester. I came up from Gloucester, and before that I was down in the Forest of Dean.'

The result was a silence, and a look of alarm on both faces, though Francis quickly mastered his.

'I went down there at the request of your father, sir,' I added, eying the man without expression. 'He asked me, as an old friend, to make enquiries into the death of his brother.'

'He did what?' With a frown, Francis Mountford sat bolt upright. 'I don't understand.'

'You will,' I replied. 'Indeed, I'm somewhat surprised that word has not yet reached you from Lydney. Are you not aware that Cricklepit Foundry has been deserted, and that production of ordnance has ceased?'

My answer was another stunned silence. But I shifted my gaze to Maria Mountford, and saw a look of horror appear. Seizing my advantage, I pressed on.

'Moreover, your foundry-master Tobias Russell is dead. He was slain while resisting arrest, on the Lydney marshes. Before he died, however, he made confession of his crimes.'

That last item was pure invention on my part, but to my satisfaction it had a profound effect: Francis Mountford rose from his chair, facing me with suppressed anger.

'You are bold, Belstrang,' he said quietly. 'Not to say, a man of surprises… is there anything more you wish to tell?'

'As it happens there is,' I answered, tapping my chest. 'I have in my possession a sworn confession from a man named Peter

Willett, which corroborates Russell's admissions.'

At that, I was startled. With a cry that was almost a yelp, Mistress Mountford got to her feet, her mouth agape.

'By the Lord Jesus!' she blurted, almost swaying where she stood. 'It's creeping out, sooner than I feared-'

'Be silent!' Her husband's command rang out harshly, at which the lady fell back into her chair as if pushed. With an effort, Mountford faced me.

'What does this mean, Belstrang?' He demanded. 'You're not a Justice now... are you here at the behest of others? You carry confessions, you say - but by what authority?'

'I'll come to that,' I said; on a sudden, I felt oddly calm. For good measure, I fumbled in my doublet and drew out one of the false statements. 'I have here another sworn admission, from a Spaniard named Sebastien,' I went on. 'I was unfortunate enough to find myself at close quarters with him, in a trow on the river. We were returning from Bristol, where I observed the unloading of a consignment of your cannons. In short, he tried to kill me - but as you can see, he failed.'

With that, I waited. From the corner of my eye, I saw Maria Mountford cast her eyes downwards in dismay. Her husband, however, appeared composed.

'Well now... you have been most assiduous,' he said, after a moment. 'And all because my father, in his confusion, asked a favour of you? Perhaps it slipped your mind when I told you he was prone to fancies, so that we even fear for his sanity?'

'Nothing has slipped my mind, sir,' I replied. 'And my journey proved most fruitful. In short, I now know that your uncle was not killed in an explosion at the foundry, for there was none. He was slain by Peter Willett, to stop his mouth after he uncovered the treachery that was being done.'

'Indeed? How interesting.' Mountford's tone was icy now. 'And by whose order do you imagine such a crime was done?'

For answer, I merely returned the man's gaze. A moment passed, whereupon he turned to his wife and, to my surprise, put out a hand to her.

'My dear, you are distressed,' he said, with a concern that was blatantly false. 'Belstrang has been precipitate in coming here with these allegations... more, he has insulted us both. I pray you, withdraw and let me deal with him.'

And with that he drew her to her feet, doubtless expecting her to make some attempt at composure and leave. In that, however, he was thwarted.

'Deal with him?' His wife echoed, in a shrill voice. 'Aye, so you shall, for you always do! What weapons will you deploy this time? Threats, bribery... a promise to drop a word in the right ear?' And to my embarrassment she turned to me, her face now flushed with bitterness.

'Have a care, Master Belstrang,' she threw out. 'You know not who you treat with. And if you accept an offer to stay here this night – as you will – then my advice is to sleep with a poniard under your pillow! That, or wield a very long spoon with which to eat your supper... God save you, sir, and good-night!'

And having said her piece – a well-delivered parting speech, I must admit – the lady turned from her husband, tugging her sleeve from his grip. Thereafter she summoned what dignity remained to her, and walked to the door without swaying once.

Yet, no sooner had she left the room than Francis Mountford faced me again, a cool smile now in place. 'Your pardon,' he said in a bland voice. 'My wife is out of sorts today... likely some woman's trouble. Yet as she intimated, I offer our hospitality - without condition. The evening draws in, and having ridden all he way from Gloucester, both you and your horse will require rest and sustenance. Dine with me, and let's see how me may move forward from this… these matters you have uncovered. I trust you will accept?'

\*\*\*

Despite everything it was rather a good supper, and I saw no reason to refuse it. It bought me time, to find means to get Francis Mountford to reveal the names of his fellow Concord Men, if that were possible. Legally, I had no powers save that of any gentleman who chose to swear out a warrant for another man's arrest. More, I was alone, and it crossed my mind more than once that Mountford could decide to take desperate measures - as he had done with his uncle, who soon featured as the chief topic of our discussion.

I had been at pains to eat no more than my fill, and to drink sparingly; tempting as Mountford's fine wines were to the palate, I had no desire to let them cloud my judgement.

'So, this man Willett confessed to killing John,' he said, as we ate our roasted capon and sallet. 'Would he be related to Jonas Willett, who once worked for us?'

'I think you know that he's his son,' I replied. 'For you loaned him money to establish his own foundry, on the Newerne stream… or had it slipped your mind?'

'Ah, yes…' Francis nodded. 'And did you meet the old man on your travels?'

'He's dying,' I said shortly. 'And in misery, now that his son's languishing in Gloucester Castle, facing the gallows.'

In truth, I was finding myself disconcerted by my host's casual manner. What was he planning? I wondered. The answer, in fact, would come later… but for now, he appeared to enjoy playing the wealthy and assured landowner.

'Appalling,' he said, with a shake of his head. 'As I recall, the son was something of a rogue. Likely we'll never know what passed between him and John Mountford.'

'You know what passed,' I said, striving to keep emotion from my voice.

'As for this Spaniard,' Francis said, as if he had not heard me, 'I confess I'm at a loss. I know no such man...'

'He went as a Turk named Yakup,' I said, cutting him short. 'He sailed with Captain Spry... the one who brought your uncle's corpse home. I might add that Spry has since fled, seeing that justice would soon be upon him. As to Yakup: after he was prevented from taking my life, I was present at his interrogation. Justice March knew a Spaniard when he saw one.'

This produced a frown, but it was quickly suppressed.

'Moreover, I spoke earlier of Tobias Russell, your foundry-master,' I continued. 'I might have said that his was not the only death that occurred down in Lydney. A man named Peck died too - also slain by Willett. But before he died, he told me something of interest. I speak now of the Concord Men.'

There, it was said. I had not intended to speak those words just yet, but I was growing weary of the discourse. Sitting back, I took a sip of wine and watched my adversary closely.

'Ah... now I see.' Francis had taken up his own cup, which he set down carefully. He was a difficult man to read, I had decided... and I was somewhat unprepared for what followed.

'You name Justice March,' he said, seemingly pondering the matter. 'And you too, of course, are a former Justice. But now, I think I see why you come here alone. For surely you did not intend to arrest me?'

I made no answer, but continued to watch him.

'After all, the motives of those wretches in the prison – Willett, and the Turk-who's-really-a-Spaniard - are unlikely to come under close scrutiny when they face trial, are they? Since as you say, both men have confessed already?'

'Perhaps you don't know Thomas March,' I replied. 'Like me, he's an old-fashioned sort who believes in retribution. He'll spare no effort in having the matter aired.'

'Provided both men come to trial,' Mountford said then. And when I tensed, he added: 'As I recall, Gloucester Castle's little more than a tumbledown ruin. All the prisoners crowded into one cell... it's not uncommon for some to perish of sickness, or even from a brawl. You understand me, I think.'

I made no reply, whereupon the man at last unsheathed the first of what his wife had called his weapons.

'Yet, in case you do not,' he added, 'I will make matters clear. At a word from me, both of those men would die. Hence, Justice March would have no trial to preside over - and those sworn confessions you claim to have would be worthless. Provided, that is, they were genuine in the first place.'

I had no answer to that. I might say that, throughout my life, I have rarely under-estimated a man's intellect, but this occasion could have been one of them. All through the meal Mountford had been calculating, and among his conclusions was that the confessions I carried were probably bogus. For he knew his hired men: the brutal Russell, the stone-hearted Yakup, and Peter Willett. Having made his opening play, he eyed me shrewdly.

'So, Belstrang,' he said at last. 'You begin to see what sort of ground you're treading, I think. As I said, you come here alone - and no doubt you value your life as much as I do mine. This... this marsh you seem to have wandered into - like the one down at Lydney - can prove to be deadly to a man who does not know the paths. Yet here you are, enjoying my table... as you will enjoy a night in the chamber that is being prepared for you. And in the morning...'

He broke off, took up a jug and refilled my cup to the brim, before topping up his own. Then he lifted it, and with a sardonic look, made a salute.

'In the morning we'll trade, shall we? Your health and

prosperity, sir - and may they both last.'

But I did not join him in the toast. And when at last I went to bed in that well-appointed chamber at Foxhill, I was prey to a confusion of thoughts as to how I might proceed on the morrow.

On the landing, guided by a servant bearing a candle, I passed the door to Sir Richard's room - but any thoughts I might have harboured about venturing in were dashed. Outside the door sat a heavy-built fellow, eying me deliberately. He wore a close-fitting hood of dark leather that covered his ears, and carried a poniard at his belt.

Inside the chamber, I sat down on the fine four-poster bed and gave way to weariness.

## SEVENTEEN

That night I had a dream, that distressed me greatly. I was at Thirldon - but I seemed to view it from a distance, from beyond the gates. As I watched, flames began to engulf the house, leaping up to the roof. Soon figures appeared at the windows, waving desperately - I recognised Childers, and Hester, and my daughter Anne. I called out in terror, but no-one seemed to hear me - then the roof began to fall in, with a terrible roaring and crashing of timbers. Unable to move, I shouted and gesticulated, knowing all was lost... whereupon I awoke in darkness, in a sweat and a panic.

Mercifully, it was no vision. Gathering my senses, I turned on my back – only to start in alarm when a voice spoke nearby.

'Peace, sir... you were but dreaming.'

It was soft and feminine, and it came from but a few feet away... was it a creak of floorboards that had awoken me? As I roused myself there came a scraping sound, a flame spurted, and in its feeble light a figure appeared, wearing what looked like a ghostly shroud. Then the flame was put to a candle on a chest by the wall, and the woman turned to face me. It was Katherine, Mistress Mountford's companion, wearing a very fetching smile.

Propped on my elbows, I gazed at her and let out a breath.

'Well now, are you going to turn back the coverlet?' She asked, taking a step closer. 'The night is somewhat chill, and I would fain be warmed... warmed, then aflame.'

And before I could utter a word, her hand went to the lacing at her neck. The gown of thin lawn fell away to reveal a most shapely body, golden in the candlelight.

'Good God...' I swallowed. 'This is absurd, mistress... do you truly intend to bed me? Why, I'm a grandfather...'

'Though a well-preserved one,' came the reply. She was at the bedside, reaching out a hand. 'Come, sir... we're but man and woman. Why not take this pleasure when it's before you?'

'One moment... you mistake,' I said, with a gulp. Tempting as the offer was, my mind was racing – and very soon, thoughts began to assemble themselves. Sitting upright, I raised a hand to stay her.

'Is it at Master Francis's behest that you came here, or his wife's?'

'What does it matter?' Katherine countered. Bending towards me, she laid a hand on my shoulder. 'No more words now. Embrace me, and let me cleave to you.'

'Wait.' Somewhat roughly, I put her hand away. 'Do you think me so pliant? This is your master's work, is it not - a gift to whet my appetite?' I drew a breath. 'And in the morning, I imagine he'll lay forth other prizes... riches, perhaps even titles that might come my way. I suspect you know what sort of man you serve.'

She made no answer, but returned my gaze without flinching. In truth, it was a difficult moment... even a man of my years has needs, which are not often fulfilled. But I forced myself to think of Hester; the dream was yet fresh in my mind.

'I pray you, clothe yourself and go,' I said at last, forcing my eyes away. 'I will forget that this occurred.'

A moment passed, then: 'You will not, sir.'

I turned sharply, aware of the change in her voice. She was gathering the smock, pulling it violently up to her neck... and as I watched, she stepped away and looked at me in anger.

'There's no fool like an old fool,' she snapped, drawing the laces tight. 'Can you not imagine what you've missed? Yet you divine aright - I would hardly throw myself upon a man like you, had I the choice. Well, grandfather, you'll find that virtue has no place at Foxhill. But when I'm gone, the sight of my body will remain with you... may you make use of it in the only way you can. Tug yourself to sleep - I leave it as my gift, and wish you sweeter dreams!'

Turning swiftly, she started for the door. But on opening it, she threw a bitter look towards me.

'As for the morning, you may find that matters fall out somewhat differently from what you expect,' she said. Then she was gone, closing the door behind her.

The sound was followed by the clatter of a key in the lock.

In an instant, I had thrown the covers aside and was on my feet - but already I had guessed my predicament. I gained the door, lifted the latch and found it immoveable. I struck it and tugged at the handle, while knowing it was futile. Finally I backed away and slumped down on the bed, gazing at the flickering candle.

I was a prisoner - and I had only my own temerity to blame. I had been a prisoner from the moment I confronted Francis Mountford and spoke of the Concord Men... perhaps from the moment I told him I had enquired into his uncle's death. It was clear as daylight: I had been offered a sop to my supposed weakness – for are all men not weak, when offered a tempting treat? And yet my suspicions – even my Puritan-like refusal too - had availed me nothing.

*No fool like an old fool*, the girl had said; and Justice Belstrang felt as big a fool as he had ever felt in his life.

\*\*\*

The morning came slowly, as slowly as it always does to those who cannot sleep. By the time the sun rose I was fully dressed, throwing back the curtains. In the distance Upton was stirring, smoke rising from chimneys, but it might have been an ocean away. I examined the lattice windows, but they were small - barely wide enough for a child to squeeze through, let alone a grown man. Even if such a man were athletic enough to try, which I was not. Agitated and consumed by anger, I went again to the door as I had done several times, rattling the handle to no avail. I even called out, but was met with silence. Finally I returned to the windows, opened them and contemplated breaking the glass. But then, who would heed my cries for help – indeed, who would even hear them? The manor stood in its own park, some distance from the road... sick at heart, I sat heavily on a stool, staring out at the birds that flitted past. Freedom is one thing I've always enjoyed, save for those grim days I once spent in the Counter in London, falsely imprisoned for debt. The memory, just then, made me rue my recent actions most pitifully.

An hour or so passed, and no-one came. I was hungry and thirsty, my temper frayed. Wild schemes had run through my mind: to try to force the door with my sword or poniard, to smash the window with a stool and shout threats... even to feign sickness, or some sort of collapse; all, of course, were absurd. Finally, I lay on the bed and tried to rest... until at last there came a jangle of keys, and the door opened.

As I expected, it was Francis Mountford who entered.

Neatly dressed as ever, and girded with a fine sword, he walked easily to the centre of the room and halted. Behind him came the ruffianly fellow in the hood, whom I had seen guarding the door to Sir Richard's chamber: a precaution, of course. Getting to my feet, I eyed my host who was now my jailer.

'Good morrow, sir... did you sleep well?' He began, assuming a thin smile. 'I can have breakfast brought in, if you wish.'

'I'll make you a promise - sir,' I said, with an effort. 'That soon you will pay for your crimes, by due process of law. I dare say your wife will make a pretty widow.'

The smile remained, however. And before I could stop myself, I had my hand on my sword-hilt... but at that, the

155

heavily-built guard stepped forward. His expression was eloquent enough: he could break my arm, he intimated, before I even drew blade.

'So,' Mountford went on, seemingly unconcerned. 'You chose to refuse the favours that were offered you last night. I'm impressed by your self-control. Few men can resist Katherine's charms... I speak from experience.'

'Let me leave here - now!' I snapped. 'This is madness. You cannot detain a man like me – a former magistrate. Moreover, Justice March knows I'm here, as does-'

Just in time, I stopped myself: something warned me not to reveal any other names. Thinking fast, I added: 'It's a reckless thing you've done, and you know it. Your schemes are uncovered, hence-'

'Hence nothing, sir,' came the sharp riposte. 'And I suggest you pay heed to me now while you can, for I'll not offer such terms again. Will you listen, or not?'

I wanted to tell the man to go hang, but on impulse I decided against it. Might this be an opportunity, I wondered, for me to get him to reveal more? Instead I forced a nod, and threw a pointed glance at the bodyguard, whereupon:

'William is stone deaf,' Mountford said, with a sigh of impatience. 'Do you still underestimate me?'

'Well, perhaps I have done,' I replied. I was making an effort to calm myself, for I saw no other solution than to humour him. 'But if you think I'm a man you can easily bribe, I should say-'

'Bribe?' Lifting his eyebrows, the other cut me short. 'Nay, sir, I would not insult you so. I speak of opportunities...' he paused, his eyes going to the window where sunlight streamed in. 'Can we not sit, and discuss terms like civilised men?'

I managed another nod. Whereupon, observed closely by the bodyguard, I moved to the window seat while Mountford caught up a stool. We sat down, each as watchful as the other.

'I will be forward with you, Belstrang,' he said, speaking quietly. 'For you've uncovered more than I would have thought you capable of... I might even applaud your diligence. But you must see that you've put yourself in mortal danger.'

I met his gaze, and waited.

'You should know that the matters you have referred to are too important to be thwarted by any man – let alone you,' he went on. 'However, I can offer you a simple choice. I suspect you know what it is.'

'You spoke of opportunities,' I said, after a moment. 'Do I take that to mean an invitation? An offer to join you and others, the-'

'*Concordia*.' Mountford's voice was flat. 'You used the term yesterday, yet I advise you not to use it again. You spoke of it with distaste, as if it were some sort of disreputable cabal. Whereas I assure you that my associates and I are simply men of business, who see where the wind blows.'

He fell silent, awaiting my response. Men like him, as I know only too well, always assume that others have their price, and merely require the right kind of inducement. Drawing a breath, I made an attempt to appear interested.

'And yet... even if I were to consider this, you understand,' I said carefully, 'you would doubtless expect some kind of investment. I'm not a man of great wealth-'

'Nor are all the others,' Mountford broke in. Was I mistaken, or did I detect signs of eagerness on this part? 'The returns are proportionate,' he went on. 'And someone who knows the workings of the law is always useful – even though there are others in our company with similar expertise.'

I must have stiffened visibly at that, for the other seemed to regret his words. 'Not that the names should concern you, Belstrang,' he added quickly. 'All you need know is that there are profits to be garnered, beyond your wildest expectations.

And so...'

Abruptly the man stood up, catching me unawares, and looked down at me. 'In short, sir, I desire an answer from you now. Work with me... join us, if you will, and you may depart from here with much to look forward to. After all...' this with a sardonic smile, that stopped short of a sneer. 'What prospects are there for an ex-magistrate of modest means, who's no longer young? You might even call this the day your fortunes changed - for the rest of your life.'

I returned his gaze. My mind was busy, yet I fumbled for the right words. Should I feign acceptance of the offer to join him and his treacherous circle, to buy more time? It would allow me to leave Foxhill, at least, whereupon I could go to the High Sheriff... yet, I was uneasy. This man was no fool, and would smell deception in an instant.

'Well, I confess you make a most powerful argument,' I said at last. 'May I ask what would happen if I spurn your offer?'

At that Mountford sighed, then fixed me with his bland look. 'Then, I fear you would shortly meet with an unfortunate accident,' he replied. 'I will be most distressed that it occurred on my land. You were enjoying the fishing, and suffered a seizure... a sudden jolt to the heart. The excitement was too much for you... with sadness, I will even show the great carp you caught in the lake, which caused your collapse.'

He paused to allow the words to sink in, then: 'As it happens, the coroner is a friend. He'll take my word as a gentleman, and direct the inquest jury to find you died of misadventure. A tragedy... but there it is.'

And there it was, stark as could be: either I joined the treacherous coterie of men who sold arms to the King's enemies, or I would lose my life. I pretended to consider, then drew a breath and rose to my feet.

'You can go to hell, sir,' I said. 'And more, you'll not fake my death by accident… I'd rather die here!'

Whereupon, startling both Mountford and his servant, I stepped back swiftly and put hand to sword-hilt: something I had resolved never to do again. I even got the blade clear of the scabbard, before stone-deaf William was upon me. With ease he took hold of my wrist, twisted it so violently I cried out, and made me let go. My basket-hilt rapier fell to the floor with a clang… and in a moment I was forced to my knees, hissing with pain as the ruffian stood over me.

A moment passed, while both men looked down. Whereupon, at a brief nod from his master, William released me and stepped away. As he did so he picked up my sword, then moved beyond my reach.

'So be it, Belstrang,' was all Mountford said. With a sigh, he turned about and walked from the room, followed by his servant. The slamming of the door was followed by the sound of the key turning once again.

And thereafter, ex-Justice Belstrang lost control, flew to the door and hammered upon it with his left hand; the right one still throbbed. Finally, wretched and breathless, I ceased my raging and slumped to the floor, cursing like a soldier… while through the open window came the startled squawking of birds.

But at the final turn, I thought later, once again I had only myself to blame. I should have feigned acceptance of Mountford's offer, and played along with his plans while I had the chance. Whether I would have convinced a man like him, however, remained in doubt.

\*\*\*

I never did get breakfast that day, nor even dinner. Instead I paced the floor of the wide chamber, berating myself for my recklessness, which had won me nothing but contempt from a man who had no more scruples than a feral cat.

It was afternoon, as I sat listlessly on the bed, before the sound of the key turning at last broke my thoughts. Rousing myself, I seized my poniard and tried to prepare for the worst… until the sight of the one who entered made me freeze.

Maria Mountford, in a blue outdoor gown, stopped by the doorway, seemingly startled by my manner. In considerable surprise myself, I watched as the lady recovered herself, before turning to the door and listening… but she did not close it.

'I will first disappoint you, sir,' she said, facing me. 'For I'm not come to offer such favours as Katherine did.'

And when I merely stared, she took a few paces forward. Getting hurriedly to my feet, I sought for some signs of her purpose – but in the next instant, I was confounded.

'And now I will scotch that disappointment,' she added. 'For I intend to be your salvation.'

## EIGHTEEN

Those last days of September, when the Great Comet finally disappeared from view, would be among the most important of my life. But I had no notion of it then, as I stood in that chamber at Foxhill and heard Maria Mountford's words. I have called Captain Darrett an unlikely saviour, but the Mistress of Foxhill should surely take the prize. In astonishment, and with mounting hopes, I listened intently... and saw my escape laid out before me.

'You will step outdoors with me,' she said. 'Some of the servants are aware of my intent, others are not. I should add that we have little time - are you ready to take a risk?'

'I am, madam,' I said warily. 'Yet I don't understand... do you mean to thwart your husband this way?'

'Pray, do not concern yourself with Francis,' came the reply. 'He is very busy just now - and in truth, that's thanks to you. He has messages to send, and people to meet with... or did you think the death of Tobias Russell, and the turmoil at Lydney, was of no concern to him?'

I remained silent.

'Nay, sir...' Mistress Mountford gave a sigh, and lowered her eyes; to my relief, she did not appear the worse for drink. 'You have kicked a wasp's nest... caused more upheaval than you know. And yet it had to come... indeed, I always knew that it would. But in any case, I suspect it's too late.'

She went to the window and looked out, then turned to face me. 'Well, shall we go? I've arranged for your horse to be saddled...' and seeing me about to reply, she lifted a hand. 'There's no time for questions. Take this chance while you may. All I ask in return is that you speak for me when... when the time comes. Will you do that?'

I gazed at her – then a notion rose that stayed me. 'Sir

161

Richard,' I said. 'I will not leave without seeing him.'

'But you must!' For the first time the lady showed unease. 'He's well enough... whatever happens, I swear no harm shall come to him. Now hurry, while you may.'

With that, she moved to the door and looked out to the landing; then she turned to me and waited. It was a difficult moment: torn between concern for my old friend and gaining my freedom, I hesitated... until with a heavy heart, I made my choice. Yet it was really no choice at all: once free of Foxhill I could ride to Sandys... surely March's letter would have reached him? While to spurn Mistress Maria's offer and remain, was but to hurry forward my death.

With a hand on my poniard's hilt, I gave a nod and followed her outside. In the deserted passage, I took a few steps and halted. We were by the door to Sir Richard's chamber, but there was no-one on guard. Sensing my delay, the lady looked round quickly.

'William has been sent elsewhere,' she said. 'He thinks I'm attending to my father-in-law, but he'll return soon - as will my husband. Please hurry.'

So: there was nothing more to be said, and I followed her quickly down the stairs. The absence of servants was striking... what deception had their mistress practised on my behalf, I wondered? We crossed the hallway, passed through a sunlit chamber, then down another passage before reaching a side door without hindrance. I thought briefly of my sword, but clearly this was not the time to try and recover it. In a moment we were outside in afternoon sunlight; I even took a moment to draw gulps of sweet air. Then, still hard upon Mistress Mountford's heels, I was hurrying through flower-beds and round a high wall, to find myself in the stable yard. Heady with relief, I looked around quickly... then stopped.

There was no sign of Leucippus.

'You said you had made arrangements…' I drew near to the lady, who also halted. 'Is it safe to go inside?'

I was eying the stable doors, which were closed… and unease was soon upon me. I looked through the archway which led to the main courtyard, but no-one was in sight.

'Wait here, please.' Somewhat taut, Mistress Mountford glanced to left and right, then started forward. Despite her instruction I followed, my hand on my poniard again. As we gained the door I put a hand out instinctively, as if to stay her. But at once it opened, and from the shadows within two figures appeared.

One was the young stable-lad, the other was William.

I stopped in alarm, then saw that the boy was dishevelled, his arms pinned behind his back. He was William's captive… and as Maria Mountford drew back in dismay, I grasped the situation. Looking past the pair, I caught a glimpse of Leucippus, saddled and bridled: the boy, at his mistress's request, had got my horse ready – but he had been waylaid.

'Let him go!' The lady shouted, making it clear with signs what she meant - but William was having none of it. He merely shook his head and indicated the boy, who spoke up.

'He came in and caught me, madam,' he said, somewhat breathlessly. 'He must have known something was going on… he's Master Francis's eyes, when all's said-'

But he broke off with a cry as his captor jerked hard on his arms, forcing them upwards. Whereupon, gathering my wits, I was obliged to act. Catching the ruffian off guard, I darted forward and snatched his poniard from his belt. Then I threw it aside – but before I could draw my own weapon the man was upon me. Shoving the stable-boy away so that he stumbled, he pushed me out into the yard and hit me on the jaw.

It was not a hard blow: the fellow knew what he did. But it was enough to make me lose my balance and fall to the cobbles

– a painful landing. Catching my breath, I looked up as he loomed above me… whereupon things started to become confusing.

I heard Mistress Maria shouting wildly – to my surprise, she had seized William's arm and was trying to pull him away. It had little effect, but the man was grunting with mingled anger and alarm… surely he would not dare to offer violence against his mistress? His gaze swung back and forth – and in that moment of hesitation I seized my chance. Scrambling aside, I drew my poniard and began to get to my feet, but I was too slow. In a second, the man had gripped my wrist and made me drop the blade, while his other hand came up, ready to knock me senseless. I was vaguely aware of the lady still shouting and tugging at him… until a loud crack silenced her.

Breathing hard, I could only watch as William staggered backwards, his arms falling to his sides. Then I saw the stable-lad behind him swinging a shovel, preparing to deal another blow, and cried out.

'Stop - move back! See to your mistress!'

His face contorted with fear – as much for what he had done, I deemed, as for what trouble he had brought upon himself – the boy dropped the shovel. William had somehow stayed on his feet… but he was dazed, blood running down one side of his face. Finally his knees weakened and he sagged… which gave me enough time to get up and grab my poniard. Dusty and winded, I threw a look towards Maria Mountford, who had drawn back open-mouthed, with the frightened boy beside her.

It was over… or so I thought. I only had to walk into the stable and lead Leucippus out, then get myself mounted. William, eyes on the ground and blowing like a carthorse, was disabled for the present… and yet I hesitated.

'What will you do?' I asked the lady. 'You have condemned yourself… do you want to leave? You can ride double with me.'

'No, sir, I cannot.'

She was shaking her head, a bleak smile on her face. Turning to the boy, she murmured a few words which sent him scurrying away. With a glance at William, she gestured me to draw close.

'I can manage my husband, Master Belstrang,' she said. 'He knows he can't silence me, not without removing me permanently – and he would not dare. As for his servant - his eyes, as the boy said - he would not accuse me even if he could speak. Do you wonder at the hood he wears? It's to cover the scars, where his ears were cropped. One further offence and he will hang... and his name's not William. He's but a hireling - an instrument, to serve Francis's whims.'

She drew a breath and gestured to the stable doors. 'Now, please get your horse and ride out while you can.'

I would have spoken, but her expression brooked no refusal. So I stepped away, picking up pace as I walked into the gloom of the stable. Leucippus was restless... at sight of me he shook his mane and came forward. Drawing alongside him, I spoke quickly but soothingly. Then I caught up the rein and led him out into the yard - only to stop in my tracks at the noise of hoofbeats.

I whirled about, towards the archway – and saw Francis Mountford riding in on a fine black horse. Behind him came two male servants in livery - and all drew rein at once, with a flurry of clattering hooves. Leucippus whinnied and stamped, as if willing me to put my foot in the stirrup... but it was too late.

'By the Christ...' Mountford eased his horse forward, to halt but a few feet away. His eyes went swiftly from me to William, then to his wife and back to me... whereupon his face twisted into a savage glare.

'Well, Belstrang, it appears you've forced matters by yourself - and rather sooner than I had planned,' he said, eying me with venom. 'Would you care to let go of the reins? Otherwise, I'll be obliged to have you shot.'

Without turning round, he jerked a thumb over his shoulder to indicate one of his servants. I looked, and saw that the man had brought a small carbine from his saddle holster, and was making it ready with speed.

With sinking heart, I dropped the rein.

\*\*\*

The next hour I find difficult to relive; not because my memory fails me, but because I recall events only too well. I see now that it could have been my last hour on earth... a vague memory of Childers and his glum words of foreboding sprang to mind. But in the end, events moved in ways I had barely hoped for... and more quickly than I expected.

The matter came to a head soon after I was disarmed by Mountford's men. Leucippus was back in the stable, William had been helped away to have his wound tended... and Mistress Maria was nowhere to be seen. Meanwhile I was marched away from the house and outbuildings by the two men who had ridden in with their master. We passed through a gate, and began to cross a field that sloped downwards - and my heart gave a thud, as I looked into the distance and saw the lake.

So: it was no idle threat. The master of Foxhill really did intend to have me despatched by the waterside - before witnesses who would doubtless swear to the manner of my death. For a moment I could almost have laughed: that fishing, one of my true passions in life, could be made the means of my losing it. Struggling to master my fear, on impulse I struck my foot on the ground and halted.

'I've a mind to be troublesome,' I said, turning to the man on my right. 'I'll go no further.'

'Your pardon, sir, but it makes no trouble,' he replied. I caught his look, and knew him for a hard rogue - the sort that Mountford employed at Cricklepit and elsewhere to do his unsavoury work. 'If need be, we'll bind you and drag you… a pity to stain your fine clothes.'

'You varlet,' I threw back, with scorn. 'Are you so dim-witted, you can't see your master is ensnared? His actions are known. There's a net closing, and anyone who aided him will-'

But I was cut short, stifled by a sweaty hand being clamped across my mouth. The two men, both angered, gripped my arms tightly.

'That's enough,' the one who had silenced me snapped. 'Go forward now or we'll carry you… the choice is yours.'

He removed his hand – whereupon I gave vent to my rage. 'Damn you!' I cried, my pulse racing. 'God knows, if I'd had you before me when I sat on the magistrate's bench, I'd have sent you both to be whipped and branded, perhaps more-'

'No - damn *you*!' The first fellow threw back, stifling me again. This time he grasped my jaw, which still ached from the blow William had dealt me… and as he squeezed, I began to struggle. Growing desperate, twisting my head this way and that, I kicked out, catching him the shins. He grunted, muttered an oath – then to my alarm shifted his grip, dropping his hand to my throat. I felt his fingers close about my windpipe, and knew this could be my last tussle… whereupon the other one spoke up.

'Stop! You know what the master's orders are. Loosen him!'

The moment that followed was so taut, I almost expected to see the two come to blows there in the field. They stood glaring at each other, with me caught in the middle. Wild notions flew up: of butting one of them, or kicking out again before making a run for it… I managed to jerk my head aside, peering round…

Then came the cataclysm.

Shouts and calls rang out, from somewhere in the direction of the house… and were those hoofbeats? I strained at my captors, who had also turned in consternation. I managed to tear one arm free, and would have struck out with it – but I did not. In amazement I saw both men step away, staring in the direction of the noise... whereupon I lunged forward, shoving one to the ground. As he fell, I turned to run to the gate.

'Here!' I shouted. 'Over here!'

Stumbling, both arms now free, I struggled to pick up pace. Since I expected to be caught from behind at any moment, I made an effort to veer sideways, first one way and then another... though out of breath, I was gaining ground. The gate was ahead; I reached it, put a hand to the latch – then stopped.

Beyond the gate lay the gardens, neatly trimmed flower beds and fruit trees. A little further off was the courtyard, which was now filled with activity. Dust was raised, and horses milled about... and still there was shouting. I saw figures – and my heart leaped at the sight of steel cuirasses, reflecting sharp sunlight. Wildly I looked round for my captors... and drew a sharp breath.

They were not behind me – in fact, they were barely in sight. They were far down the field, sprinting at full tilt... and as I gazed, they split apart to take different courses. With heart pounding, I leaned against the gate and slumped.

They were running for their lives - while mine was saved.

And moments later I was walking exhaustedly into the courtyard... where, at sight of the only man I recognised, I halted and let out a breath.

'Sir Samuel?'

Sir Samuel Sandys, the High Sheriff of Worcestershire, turned in surprise. He was somewhat flushed, grey hair plastered to his brow with sweat... yet for a man in his fifties, he had always been agile. With raised brows, he lifted a hand and started towards me.

'Belstrang? What in God's name are you doing here?'

'Just now, sir, I'm thanking God for your timely arrival,' I answered. 'You are come at the eleventh hour - I could say at the last minute of that hour. If I said "well met", it would fall somewhat short.'

Whereupon I took another step, and clasped his hand warmly.I no longer felt pain… only a blessed sense of relief.

## NINETEEN

The afternoon became evening, and as night fell candles were brought into the main parlour of Foxhill by subdued servants. Three of us sat at the table, weary yet calm, to slake our thirst and eat a little food. One was Sir Samuel Sandys, I was another... and the third was Sir Richard Mountford.

He was pale and haggard, so that I berated myself silently for intending to leave him. But his mind was clear, despite the distressing news he had been obliged to hear: that his own son had not only betrayed him by trading illicitly, but had bespoken the death of John Mountford. It would have been hard for any man to bear. Now he sat in silence; he ate nothing, only taking sustenance from a hot posset that had been brought. Matters had been aired between us, almost to the point of exhaustion; the truth was not pretty, but at least it was out.

Seeing that he should take charge, the High Sheriff spoke up with his natural authority.

'I had word some days ago from Justice March, in Gloucester,' he said. 'He acted rightly and promptly – as have you, Belstrang. Even if your innate recklessness got you into trouble, once again.'

He paused to drink, then eyed Sir Richard. 'In God's name, sir, I heartily wish you spoken to me of your suspicions, however vague. Now a nest of vipers has been uncovered – these Concord Men.' He shook his head, and turned to me.

'The list of names is long – and some of those on it confound me. Papists I might have expected, in view of the unfolding business on the Continent. But others are noblemen, merchants, men I trusted... some of them known to you. The late Giles Cobbett was among them.'

At that I showed my surprise: Cobbett, whose vile abuse and slaying of his own daughter I had helped uncover the year before... the greedy landowner, whose wealth was never enough.

'You know all of them, then?' I asked. 'The names?'

Sandys nodded. 'Your son has turned tell-tale, now that all is up,' he said to Sir Richard. 'Though I would be dishonest, were I to say that there's any hope of him cheating the gallows. It's a very grave matter. I can but offer you my sympathy, and my heartfelt condolences.'

I glanced at Sir Richard, and was saddened: he looked a beaten man. He was holding his mug as if to warm his hands... and I saw them shake. He made no answer, but gazed down at the table. We were all silent for a while. I knew Francis had been confined to his chamber soon after Sandys' arrival, and had been questioned at length. In the end he had babbled to try and save his own skin, which did not surprise me.

'Your daughter-in-law... Mistress Maria,' I ventured, at which Sir Richard looked up; the lady, I should add, was conspicuous by her absence, and had retired to her rooms. 'I know she is not blameless, yet she tried to aid me,' I said. 'She has been foolish, perhaps...'

But I trailed off as my friend shook his head.

'Nay, Robert - I pray you, don't excuse her. She chose to wed my son, knowing what sort of a man he was... he promised her riches, and made good on his promise.' He let out a great sigh. 'The foundries always paid well... we were productive and respected by all, including the King. Why in heaven's name could Francis not have been content with that?'

There was no answer. Turning the matter over, I found myself pitying Maria Mountford, as I pictured her trying in vain to pull the ruffian William away from me. That one's fate was already sealed: he was in irons under guard, and would be taken to the prison at Worcester. He was a wanted man, it transpired, and would pay the highest price.

I emerged from my reverie, for Sandys was speaking. 'In truth, I have no cause to take your kinswoman into custody, Sir Richard,' he said. 'You will make your own choices. It may be that you will be called as a witness in time, but-'

He broke off, as on a sudden Sir Richard banged a hand down on the table. And I was heartened at once, for I detected a spark in his eye. He was not yet himself, but somehow he would rise from this mire… I saw it, and rejoiced.

'In God's name, I'm just beginning to see how much I must do,' he said fiercely. 'I have been a fool and a milksop. I let Francis take decisions - I even allowed that damned physician to advise me. As for Maria and that companion of hers, they shall be separated. I never trusted the woman. Indeed, I believe I will have to look afresh at every one of my servants, and see whom I wish to keep.'

'The stable-lad,' I murmured, after a moment. 'He too tried to aid me… he is courageous.'

Sir Richard met my eye, and to my relief gave a nod. I found my mind drifting to Katherine, and her startling night-time visit to my bedside; yet I found no sympathy for her.

'Indeed, we all have much to do,' Sandys said, growing brisk. 'Warrants have gone out for the conspirators – I use the term advisedly – to be taken and confined. As for the shipments of ordnance…'

'In that matter, Sir Samuel, I beg you to give me leave to act,' Sir Richard broke in. 'As soon as I may, I will ride down to Dean and begin to set matters to rights. When the foundry reopens, it will be under a master I can trust.'

He hesitated, then: 'Somehow, I will have to make amends to the King for what's occurred. If he considers me to blame, then I must answer the charges.'

'Well, I'll do what I can in that regard,' Sandys told him. 'My report will soon be in the hands of the Chief Justice. Yours,

Belstrang' - this with an approving glance at me – 'I have already read, as you know. In truth, I would not be surprised if some acknowledgement comes your way in time, for what you did. I will not say *reward*... doubtless you are aware of the King's partial manner in bestowing favours.'

But despite the warmth of his tone, at that a gloom fell upon me. In the turmoil of recent days, I had managed to put aside my fears about losing Thirldon. On a sudden, I was most eager to return.

'May I ride back to Worcester with you in the morning, sir?' I asked. 'I have urgent business at home, and have been away too long.'

'Of course.' The High Sheriff was eying me, as if turning some matter over. Finally, he said: 'There is a name on the list of Concord Men that will be of interest to you. In truth, it came as a shock to me... a man I had considered a friend. You will know whom I speak of: he holds the post of Justice of the Peace, as well as acting coroner.'

I stiffened, drawing a quick breath... and in an instant, a jumble of thoughts fell into place.

Standish... of course.

A memory sprang up, of Francis Mountford telling me how the coroner was a friend of his, who would direct a jury to give a verdict of misadventure upon my demise... I met the High Sheriff's eye, but remained silent.

'We'll speak of it on the journey homewards,' he said, with a nod. Facing Sir Richard, he added: 'We must prevail on your hospitality this night, before taking our leave early. It's not far, but time is short. In truth, I fear that certain of those men - the Concord Men, to use their own name - may be planning to escape. If indeed, they have not done so already.'

It was another sobering thought... whereupon, still collecting my wits, I seized upon a notion. 'Might I beg a favour of you,

Sir Samuel?' I asked. 'That I be present when you send men to Justice Standish? I have some personal matters to see to-'

'No, sir.' The riposte was sharp, cutting me short. 'I'll not be a party to the settling of old scores. Half of Worcestershire knows of your feud with Standish. He'll get his deserts, but in the proper manner.'

I made no reply. In truth, despite everything the thought of Matthew Standish ending his days on the end of a hangman's rope was not something I relished. I took a drink, and found Sir Richard's gaze upon me.

'I have much to thank you for, Robert,' he said with a sigh. 'In truth, had I known what I asked, I should never have begged your intervention in the matter of John's death. Though you have brought some small relief: to know that his body was not ruined by any explosion is a comfort. We will hold a service for him in the church in Upton... I may even raise a monument.'

He thought for a moment, then: 'As for those rogues down at Lydney – Russell's death is no more than he deserved. Though in truth I used to trust him, as I did Spry and others...' he lowered his gaze. 'What a cauldron of wickedness was brewed. I will forever blame myself for letting John – a man as trusting as he was upright and fair – go down there on my behalf. He uncovered the treachery, but perished for it.'

Silence fell again, and this time it was not broken. Having said all that he wished for the present, Sandys rose, saying he had matters to attend to before retiring. His men – guards from the county militia - were being fed in the Foxhill kitchens before going to their billets in the outbuildings.

Just then, the manor was become a garrison.

I watched the High Sheriff go, then stood up myself... and to my surprise, I swayed a little. It was a timely reminder of my age, and of the fact that engaging in tussles with armed ruffians was something I should hence refrain from, forever. Had I not made some similar resolve already, back on the salt-marshes at Lydney? My memory was vague on the matter. I only knew that I ached in several places, not least my jaw. Recovering myself, I murmured something about a touch of vertigo, and told Sir Richard I would go to take my rest.

'When a little time is passed, I beg you will return,' he said, making the effort to rise himself. 'You and your family are forever welcome. Yet I will understand if you choose not to accept the invitation.'

But I met his eye, and nodded. 'Of course I'll visit. Hester and I would be glad of it.'

'God bless you, Robert,' was all he said. Whereupon I managed a tired smile and left him at his table. The knight and loyal subject of the crown had quitted his chamber of confinement, and was master of his estate once again.

But he would have no heir to succeed him: the bitterest pill a man may swallow.

***

I did not see Sir Richard again for a long while, and I need not speak of it now. Nor did I see Mistress Maria, or her companion. Along with Sir Samuel and his eight or nine men, I took my leave of Foxhill early in the morning as a mist rose from the Severn. Summer was passing, and the air was chill. The last person I spoke with was the young stable lad: another of my rescuers. It gave me pleasure to put money in his hand, and to observe his pride when I commended his courage.

Thereafter, I mounted Leucippus and at last rode out of the stable yard, across the courtyard to the manor gates. Behind Sandys and myself rode a tight-knit party with two prisoners in their midst: William, dull-eyed, with head hanging... and Francis Mountford, staring ahead as if unconcerned at his plight. But I had caught his eye when he was brought from the house, and knew him for the dissembler he was. He suffered - and to his chagrin, he saw that I knew it.

His wife, as I had told him in anger, would indeed make a pretty widow.

Two hours of steady riding, and we reached Worcester – and seldom have I been so glad to pass through the Sudbury Gate and enter the old city. It was a Thursday, the streets were a-bustle and the cries of hawkers assailed me. I would have taken time to drink it all in before taking a welcome mug at the Old Talbot, but an urgency was upon me. Thirldon awaited, as did Hester and Childers... what news might also await me, I tried not to think upon.

Around mid-day, with the Minster bells clanging, I at last took leave of Sir Samuel. The High Sheriff's home was at Ombersley, north of the city, but he had much to do here. Having seen William taken off to the Castle prison, he sat his horse and faced me. Francis Mountford remained mounted nearby, guarded closely but unbound. He was still a nobleman, and would be found suitable accommodation in the house of some city worthy before he came to trial.

'At the final turn, Belstrang, I find myself short of words,' Sir Samuel said at last. 'I would commend you, but it seems inadequate. Rest assured that The Chief Justice – and His Majesty too – will hear the whole of what has been done. I will write to Justice March too, in Gloucester; a choleric gentleman, I always thought - as impetuous as you. But his heart is true, as is his passion for justice... you are rare beasts, the two of you.'

Whereupon he offered his hand, which I took readily. And we parted, wheeling our mounts: Sandys for the Guildhall and I for the West Gate, to take the road to my treasured estate. It was but weeks since I had left, yet it seemed like a year.

I shook the reins, felt Leucippus respond - then on a sudden impulse I halted, causing him to blow his nostrils in irritation.

The notion had flown to my mind again, as it had the evening before at Sir Richard's table. For a moment, I sat in the saddle while the people of Worcester surged about me… then I made my decision.

Was it rash, foolish, or merely sentimental? To this day, I do not know. All I can say is that I turned Leucippus and urged him away in the opposite direction. A few minutes later I had ridden to the door of Matthew Standish's fine house, where I dismounted. I looked about for a boy to hold my horse, but saw only a ragged, barefoot girl, eying me impertinently. With a sigh, I made my request and held out the coin, which she accepted with a ready smile.

And yet I did not return it; my heart was aflutter with mingled anger, anticipation and… what, fear? No matter: in a moment I had ascended the steps and knocked firmly on the door. From habit – for so it had become of late - I put my hand on my sword, feeling the reassuring coldness of its steel hilt. I had spared no effort to retrieve it, back at Foxhill.

The door soon opened, and the familiar face of Standish's servant appeared. At sight of me he blinked in surprise, then put on an apologetic look.

'The Justice is at dinner, sir,' he murmured. 'Though if you care to wait a while, I'll inform him of your coming.'

'Do so,' I said. 'As for my waiting, I expect there will be no need. Tell him I'm come from the Forest of Dean, on a matter of great importance.'

With raised eyebrows, the servant nodded. Once admitted, I made my way into the wide hallway, stopping before the door to Standish's private closet: the scene of a number of verbal debacles between him and I. While I waited, I took a moment to try to straighten my appearance. I was painfully aware of how scuffed and bedraggled I appeared, after recent adventures. And yet, why should it matter now? Soon I was scolding myself, and working up a degree of anger in the process. It did not abate as the Justice himself appeared - somewhat soon, to my satisfaction. Indeed, he was still wiping his mouth with a napkin as he came up, before stopping with a frown.

'We have business, you and I,' I said shortly. 'And it will not wait... shall we go in?'

## TWENTY

It took less time than I expected to lay the entire matter forth. By the time I had finished Standish was seated behind his cluttered table, gazing downwards. The meeting had begun with the two of us on our feet, but after the truth emerged in all its starkness, he had slumped down heavily.

'There you have it – Master Justice,' I said. 'I suspect you have a very short time to settle your affairs... perhaps only an hour or two. I would advise alacrity.'

He looked up then, and fixed me with a look of bafflement. 'In God's name, why do you do this?' He said at last. 'You and I are enemies... we've been at daggers drawn for years. I cannot divine your purpose.'

'My purpose?' I echoed. 'In truth I haven't thought on it much, beyond salving my own conscience. I may despise you – and a part of me would like to see you hauled away in irons – yet we go back a long way. As I recall, you were not always such an avaricious man... then, that was before you married.'

I let that hang in the air, whereupon he looked away. A memory flew up, of Dorothy Standish and her foppish companion mocking me in the street, the day that Hester and I went to see the play of *Faustus*. I confess that it caused me no regret, to think of what might lie ahead for that woman.

'Good Christ... I must think.'

On a sudden Standish was on his feet, as if the urgency of the situation had only now struck home. *An hour or two*, I had said: the man's agitation grew as I watched.

'I... I know not what to say to you,' he mumbled. His gaze wandered about the room: along the bookshelves where his fine library rested, to the portrait of his father who had also been a magistrate. I had never thought to pity this man but, thinking on what lay ahead of him, I almost did. At the least, my pent-up anger was gone. Taking up my hat, I turned to go out, then paused.

'What will you do?' I asked. 'Or rather, where will you go?'

'My son... he has a small estate in Ireland,' came the answer. 'Meath... I hear it's wild and bleak, but...' he spoke absently, his mind elsewhere. Then he stiffened and looked up sharply. 'I beg you to forget that. It's only a notion... I must think.'

'Perhaps you should,' I replied.

And I left him: an agitated figure, scarcely knowing which way to turn.

I have said that, to this day, I do not know why I did what I did. I had allowed a man guilty of corruption to evade capture and certain execution. I had also taken revenge, of a sort. But in so doing I had torn off the burr that had chafed me for years, and felt relief. Standish faced an uncertain, nay a desperate future... if indeed he had a future at all.

It would serve. I only hoped that no-one would suspect me of being the one who gave him the chance to take flight.

As I left the house under the uncertain eyes of the servant, a voice floated from the main parlour. Dorothy Standish was still at dinner... what words she would utter when she heard what had to be done, I did not care to think on.

In the street, I paid off my barefoot horse-holder and took up the reins; in her care, Leucippus appeared docile enough. I favoured the child with a smile before getting myself mounted, watched her walk away... and then the weight descended again: the one that had first settled on me that day at Thirldon, when George's letter had brought such dismay.

A half hour later, as the afternoon drew on, I at last rode through the gates and into the courtyard, where I saw my groom Elkins carrying a bale of hay from the stable. At sight of me he started, then dropped the bale and hurried forward.

'By heaven, sir,' he exclaimed. 'We thought something bad

had happened. Mistress Hester got a letter, said you were in some trouble…'

'I'm perfectly well, Elkins,' I lied. Dismounting stiffly, I handed him the reins. 'This fellow needs a good rub down, a meal and a long rest. He's had some hard usage of late. Will you do your utmost?'

'I will, sir.' He grinned cheerfully. Seemingly, I reflected, at least there had been no grim news to trouble the servants… I started for the house, then paused.

'What tidings?' I asked. 'Has anything occurred in my absence?'

'Tidings?' He scratched his head. 'No… well, one of the mares lost a shoe. I meant to get the farrier in…'

But seeing me walk off, he ceased his prattle.

I entered the house and found everything serene; not the homecoming I had feared. Was this to the good, or not? Stiff from riding, sweaty and dusty, I made my way to the kitchens. Here at least, there was activity: two or three wenches started at sight of me and bobbed quickly. Finally Henry appeared, a look of surprise on his face.

'Welcome back, Master Justice. We didn't know when you would come, so…'

'I'm thirsty,' I told him. 'Will you get me a drink? And would someone run and tell Mistress Hester I'm here?'

One of the maids went out at once, whereupon I slumped down at the big table, cluttered with bowls and knives and vegetables to be chopped. I needed to wash and change my attire… likely I stank, I realised. When Henry brought me a mug of ale, I drank it down in one gulp.

'Any news, while I've been gone?' I asked.

'Nothing of any moment, sir. I've some trout and a goose for supper, if you will… and a tansy pudding, and-'

'Excellent,' I said, without interest. I got to my feet and

moved towards the door, just as the maid came hurrying back.

'Mistress Hester awaits you, sir... she's most happy that you're returned safe.'

I nodded and went out. Still in my boots, I tramped towards my private closet, whereupon Hester appeared at once. I halted, searching her expression, but saw only a smile of welcome. We embraced warmly, and for longer than was our habit. But when I released her, her face was grave.

'There's a letter from George,' she said quietly. 'It came more than a week ago... I didn't dare to open it.'

I drew a breath and followed her into the room. There were papers on my table, bills requiring attention. But Hester had been discreet: the letter from George was shut in my iron coffer, away from the eyes of any servant who might come in to sweep the floor. I brought it forth, and we both sat down. Whereupon I opened it hastily, unfolded it and read.

'Well?' Even Hester could barely contain her impatience. 'What has he to say?'

I did not answer, but read the whole letter again before lowering it... and shook my head.

'Nothing good,' I said, my spirits sinking. 'He has tried his utmost to petition the King, as I knew he would. Badgering courtiers and secretaries... he even rode into Surrey to waylay the Royal Progress, but was unable to gain audience. All he could discover was that the King appears set on purchasing Thirldon. Needless to add, nobody has any inclination to try and persuade him otherwise.'

I looked aside, a great weariness upon me; just then I could have cursed James Stuart and his preening favourite Buckingham to the very devil. Then footsteps sounded outside, and Childers entered.

'Master Justice...' he managed a smile. 'What a relief to see you returned. Not having much news, we feared...' But seeing my expression he stopped short, his eyes going to the letter. Then he faced Hester, who merely shook her head.

And thereafter the three of us were silent, taking in the stark reality in our own ways: as I had feared all along, Thirldon must be given up. It was merely a matter of when.

\*\*\*

The days that followed were suffused with gloom; I know no other way to put it. While I spent much of the time in my closet dealing with correspondence, Hester went about her business of managing the house. But our despondency grew difficult to conceal: quite soon, we both knew I must call the entire household together and tell them what would happen.Childers, meanwhile, appeared his usual dour self, which attracted no attention at all.

But I knew what a burden he bore, and it seared my heart. The Sabbath came and went, and I knew he prayed fervently for some change of fortune; being a sceptic, I held out no such hope. On the following day, accepting that I could delay no longer, I was taking a turn in the garden before dinner when a horseman arrived. Suspecting the worst, I hurried to the courtyard to find Childers speaking with the messenger, who had dismounted.

'It bears the royal seal,' Childers said, somewhat hoarsely. He pointed to an important-looking packet, which the horseman had produced from inside his coat. As I approached, the man made his bow and held it forth. He was indeed wearing royal livery.

'It comes from Windsor, sir,' he said, 'where His Majesty has retired after his Progress. I was ordered to make haste, and deliver it into your own hands.'

I exchanged a glance with Childers, then took the packet. Yet, being almost certain of what its contents were, I was loth to open it. Delaying shamelessly, I bade the messenger go to the kitchens and relay my instruction, that he be given food and drink. But the man shook his head.

'I would first see you open it, sir – you, and no other. Those are my orders.'

'Indeed?' Now as tense as Childers was, I hesitated further, but it was no use. There in the courtyard I broke the seal, unfolded the paper and read… and read again, blinking… then looked up.

'Master Justice?' Childers looked aghast; naturally he assumed all was lost, until:

'It's good tidings,' I said, somewhat shakily. 'Indeed, it's surprisingly good tidings… as welcome as they are unforeseen. We'll go indoors…' I turned to the messenger, and drew a breath.

'Take your dinner now,' I urged him. 'And when you're ready to leave, I'll have a reply ready for you to carry.'

He bowed again, and when Childers pointed the way, walked off. I turned to go into the house, but felt a tug on my sleeve.

'Sir, I'm all a-quiver. What's the message? Tell me now!'

In truth, I was still taking it in. Only minutes ago, I had feared my world was soon to collapse; now, however… I took a breath, and faced him.

'It seems I am to be knighted,' I said. 'The King bids me come to Windsor - and bring my wife.' And when the other stared, I made haste to reassure him.

'As for Thirldon, you may take heart – as may we all. By His Majesty's good grace and favour, in reward for certain services rendered in the matter of… I'll not quote the entire passage. In short, he'll make other plans with regard to my estate, which he gives me leave to enjoy in perpetuity.'

I paused, then added: 'What a generous monarch… *good grace and favour*. Do you mark that?' And a smile came upon me then, as relief seemed to fill the very air about us. Childers, however, was almost speechless.

'Bring your wife?' He echoed vaguely. 'How will that fadge?'

'Come inside,' I said. 'And summon Mistress Hester, if you will. I suspect we'll all need a strong drink.'

And at last, the tension seemed to drain from Childers, as if seeping into the very cobbles beneath his feet. A smile appeared; he heaved a sigh, then nodded. As we began to walk, he paused and lifted his face to the sky.

'The Great Comet disappeared some days ago,' he said. 'I did think that our troubles might pass with it, though in truth I was losing hope. But I was wrong… and I swear, I'll never lose hope again as long as I'm alive.'

Whereupon I patted his arm, and led the way indoors.

## TWENTY-ONE

My plans were soon in train to ride to Windsor, where I would become Sir Robert Belstrang. It was a time of joy, even as October arrived with wind and showers of rain. And on a sudden there seemed a great deal to do: letters to write, people to inform, and not least a new suit of clothes to be ordered. In some haste, I called my tailor out from Worcester and spent a fraught hour or two agreeing styles as well as terms, with Hester in attendance. By the time the man had gone I was irritable, but calmed myself with a cup of Rhenish in my parlour.

And here at last, I made my proposal.

It had been on my mind for days, ever since the King had kindly invited me to bring my wife with me on the day of ceremony. Several other men were to be knighted along with me: the usual practice. How many of them had chosen to purchase their titles, of course, I could not know – again, a common practice. Hence, I confess to a degree of satisfaction in knowing that I had earned my reward, for services to the Crown. Clearly, Sir Samuel Sandys had been as good as his word and spoken well of me, with regard to what had occurred down in the Forest of Dean, and at Bristol and thereafter.

I had emerged from a nightmare: one filled with danger and devilry - or merely plain greed and deception. Such comprise the daily fare of magistrates, and I suspect they always will... but I digress. I must come to the last part of my tale, which warms my heart as I relate it.

There was never any doubt as to whether Hester would agree to becoming the future Lady Belstrang. She had never touched upon the topic, being most loyal to her late mistress; yet in my heart, I knew Margaret would have been glad. When I finally spoke to her alone, she accepted with good grace. She made no remark about the years she had waited to be asked – nor about the gossip that had swirled about us both during that time.

And so, in the end it was a matter of relief to us both. Moreover, although we knew our wedding must wait a while, I insisted upon her accompanying me to Windsor as my bride-to-be. Let tongues wag as they may, the future Sir Robert said. Meanwhile, the news was soon out at Thirldon, and not a soul was displeased - or even surprised very much. Whatever had been said behind closed doors, I chose not to think on.

But there is one matter of great importance yet to relate. On the very evening before our leaving to take the long ride to Windsor – the best part of a hundred miles, a journey we would break at Oxford – I received a letter from Ombersley, a few miles away. Knowing it to be from the Sir Samuel Sandys, I half-expected to be summoned as a witness in a trial, perhaps that of Francis Mountford.

But I was mistaken.

We were at supper - Hester, Childers and I – when the message was brought by my servant Lockyer. In some irritation at being distracted from a meal of celebration, I took a fortifying drink before opening it. Yet, when I finally perused the elegantly-written letter, I was confounded.

'Nothing unfortunate I hope, Master Justice?' Childers enquired warily. His resolve to be of better cheer these days, I might say, had proved as fleeting as I expected. With raised eyebrows, I dropped the letter on the table and met his gaze.

'Not at all,' I replied. 'Indeed, I might say it's most fortunate, save that fortune has played but a small part in it.' And when both he and Hester waited in anticipation, I laid it forth.

'You know that Matthew Standish left Worcester somewhat precipitately,' I said. 'Hence, I am invited to return to the magistrate's bench in his place... temporarily, of course. It seems there's been correspondence between the Chief Justice and the High Sheriff, as well as the Council... but no matter.

Sandys is clear enough: his wish is that I remain in the post for as long as I choose. In short, until I become infirm or start falling asleep in court... you may speculate at will.'

I looked up, and found both of them gazing at me as if struck dumb.

'By heavens, what wondrous news...' Childers was the first to find voice. Shaking his head, he lifted his cup and called for a toast: to the man who would once again be Justice Bestrang.

'Justice *Sir* Robert,' Hester corrected. 'Soon to be, anyway.' But she too lifted her silver cup, and threw me a smile that spoke a great deal.

'And what good timing,' she added, as we all drank. 'After all that's passed of late, I was beginning to fear that your weakness for throwing yourself into other people's troubles was becoming a habit, if not a compulsion. In truth, being an ex-magistrate has proved more tiresome – and more dangerous - than being a serving one. Would you not agree, sir?'

'Perhaps,' I replied. But as the truth sank home, I found myself somewhat lost for words. Childers' phrase was yet in my mind: I would once again be Justice Belstrang.

Later - some weeks later – I would make another decision: that I would set the tale of the past three years down on paper: a sort of private chronicle, if you will, of events that had begun with my Year of Astonishment. But just then, with the prospect of a long ride on the morrow, I was content to experience a feeling of deep calm, and to drain my cup.


Outside, the wind was getting up; but inside Thirldon a good fire burned, and a warm glow stole over me. Further toasts were proposed: I might even have said *God save the King*, but restrained myself without too much difficulty.

And now at last, I am done.

*

Printed in Great Britain
by Amazon